MW00477798

Born in the 1980s

Editor: Catherine Browne

route 21

First published by Route
PO Box 167, Pontefract, WF8 4WW
info@route-online.com
www.route-online.com

ISBN (13): 978-1-901927-40-5
ISBN (10): 1-901927-40-7

Editor:
Catherine Browne

Support:
Rob Brearley, Nat Clifford, Ian Daley, Isabel Galan,
Bela Gligorova, Manuel Lafuente, Oliver Mantell,
Steven Newman, Emily Penn, Emma Smith.

Cover Design, Art Direction and Photography
made in The Designers Republic
www.thedesignersrepublic.com

A catalogue for this book is available from the British Library

All rights reserved
No reproduction of this text without written permission

Printed in the UK by CPI Bookmarque, Croydon, CR0 4TD

Route is supported by Arts Council England

Stories

'Next phase, next stage, next grade, next wave.'

The Spice Girls, Pepsi 'Next Generation' campaign

'They Don't Care About Your Ad,
They Care What Their Friends Think.'

www.readwriteweb.com

Christopher Robin Is Cold

Luis Amate Perez

'All we need to get started is a suggestion.'

The audience takes a moment. To swallow? To twist off a cap from one of the light beers they've brought? To be clever?

Forty in attendance (give or take), but only one, somewhere in the back row, way beyond the reach of the stage lights, speaks up. Two syllables, the first of which hangs like the string of saliva your big brother would dangle over your contorting face. The voice in the back row chuckles and the last syllable lands, gooier than any spit glob: *Breakup.*

'The suggestion is BREAKUP!'

★

RENE

The four capital letters stayed in my cell phone directory until a week ago. Until their erasure, I had tried to draw out every one of Rene's rings and vibrations – six months had passed before she pointed out the misspelling of her name.

'Where's the other *e*?' she asked, her lips stained purple from our four-dollar bottle of Californian red. Bob

Dylan's 'Lay Lady Lay' played and I sat reasonably drunk on the hardwood floor, massaging her calves. I loved what years of soccer had done to those legs! She turned on my leather loveseat, 'Do you think I'm a *boy*?'

'I know you're not a boy,' I said, running my lips from the word 'wish' on her ankle to the elastic edges of her pink thong.

'Don't kiss my butt!'

I sank my teeth into her tush, making sure to wipe the spittle before going to work on her thighs. She continued to examine the contents of my phone – out of what I hope was jealousy.

'Ooh, who's Sharon? Victoria?...Are you *cheating* on me?'

'Isn't that what we're doing right now? Cheating?'

'That's not funny.'

My palate was dry, so I went to the kitchen, ran the faucet water over my tongue, wishing the water were wine. I turned off the faucet and got a Budweiser from the fridge. Belle and Sebastian's 'If You're Feeling Sinister' was playing for my re-entrance.

'What are you doing?'

'Trying to fix my name,' she said as she sat up, her fingers panicking on the phone's buttons.

'Don't *fix* it! There's nothing to fix.'

'Every other girl in your phone's spelled right.'

I took the phone from her. 'You don't even know what the hell you're doing.' I scanned it, making sure all was in order. She took the Bud from my hand and guzzled half of it. I put the phone on my desk, and snuggled my face into her lap. She ran her dampened fingers through my hair, scratching the back of my neck with her short, unpainted nails.

'What are we doing, Rene?'

'I have a pretty name…'

'Prettier than mine.'

'…and I don't want you to forget how pretty I am…'

'Prettier than me.' I lifted up her grey t-shirt (one of the many she'd annexed from my closet) and pressed my lips to the roll in her tummy.

'…and you can't make love to a girl named *Rene* – with just one *e* – because then it's like you're making love to a boy…'

I kissed each hard, smooth thigh, and then I looked into her sleepy, brown eyes. 'You're not a boy, you're a pretty, pretty girl, and you're Rene with one *e* because I can't spell for shit, but you're *my* Rene with one *e* and nobody else's. Remember that.'

'I had too much wine,' she smiled. Her purple-stained teeth looked false.

I licked them, trying to get drunker. 'You gonna stay with me?'

'I can't tonight.'

★

Everything finds its way onto the stage.

In Improv, the suggestion will shock your mind into motion, reviving it from its otherwise detached walk over to the black box theatre on East 4th Street. Whether you like it or not – or realise it – you'll start associating events (Mr. Fitzpatrick's wake, a Halloween Party, the first time you made love) with the suggestion: *Breakup*. The words will have numerous connotations (hysteria, drunkenness, infidelity) and bring to mind so many traumatic specifics (the word 'wish' tattooed on an ankle, an 8' x 10' room full of Winnie the Pooh paraphernalia, dried blood on your moustache). These are the things that make scenes.

But I'm not the only one on stage. *Breakup* has an infinite number of meanings for the other members of The Baldwins. We each have our own first line to initiate the first scene, but I'm the quickest off the backline. I sit down in a chair, affecting a shiver, and say in my most delicate, child-sensitive voice possible: 'Oh Christopher Robin, it is so very cold!'

The audience reacts to my impersonation with a few titters, while I attempt to tacitly script the rest of the action to come:

Enter **CHRISTOPHER ROBIN**. *He looks at a quaking* **POOH** *with horrified eyes. Christopher Robin realises what he must do in order to survive the Arctic winter.*

POOH *unintentionally rubs his russet fur. He has already licked the dregs of honey from his paws. A singular patch of hair falls to the cold floor. He tries to understand Christopher Robin's survival instinct – that this moment of separation was bound to come. Pooh scans the icy grotto, looking for the words to save the both of them.*

POOH: My poor friend Christopher Robin. It is so very cold and you are only wearing shorts and a Polo shirt. I wish it were summer. I wish we were *not* in the Arctic. Then you would not have to skin me – but I am so very small, Christopher Robin! You will not even get a hat out of me!

CHRISTOPHER ROBIN (*in tears*): Pooh!

POOH: Christopher Robin, I am so very small…

But when Christopher Robin, as played by Dan, *does* break from the backline, the scene changes drastically: the icy walls of the grotto melt away to reveal the bare stage.

'Damn it, Pooh!' Christopher Robin says, pissed off. 'You know that you're supposed to handle all of the bills. It was your job to pay the heating bill… Now what the hell did you do with the money?'

Pooh, no longer fearing the skinning knife, responds: 'I bought honey with it.'

The first big laugh comes, and Christopher Robin waits to deliver his next line: 'I knew it! Piglet told me not to trust you. Here I am, believing that you quit the junk, and then you go behind my back and cop honey – with *my* money!'

'I'm sorry, *baby*,' Pooh says, pawing at Christopher Robin's shoulder. 'This is my last time, I swear.'

'I've heard this all before, Pooh.'

In a later scene, Christopher Robin, Tigger, Piglet, and Rabbit will organise an intervention, but ultimately Pooh will overdose in the last scene of the night, succumbing to the same fate as his fellow user, manic depressive Eeyore.

The audience eats it up.

★

We were always drunk. I don't think Rene and I ever needed a sober moment. We had first met at a wake – well, at Donovan's Pub after a wake. Mr Fitzpatrick had suffered a myocardial infarction. I was childhood friends with his son Walter, and Rene had dated Walter when she was at Binghamton. Walter had been a nice weekend screw, she'd tell me minutes after I'd dropped my line on her: *You know, I was gonna wear that dress tonight. I'm glad I didn't though. That would've been so embarrassing.*

'That is the worst pickup line I've ever heard,' she laughed. 'Are you wearing *Reeboks*? Those are the *worst*!'

I defended the honour of my sneakers, using words like 'hip' and 'dig'. I dug her right away. I liked her dress too, a black number that fell a little above the knee, her cleavage inviting.

'Are you looking at my tits now?'

'Yes.'

She wore her hair pulled (always) into a ponytail, a few deviant strands behind her left ear. She was drinking Woodpecker cider that afternoon, and bought me a Corona. She handled the lime for me, pushing the wedge through the mouth of the bottle until it broke the surface of the beer. She handed me the bottle, then ran her thumb once over my lips.

'Thank you,' I said. I can still taste the lime.

The pub – it wasn't even three o'clock yet – looked like Happy Hour in Midtown. Mr Fitzpatrick's mourners crammed against each other, and someone's dollar bill found the jukebox. James's 'Laid' was the first song to hit the air and Bon Jovi's 'Livin' on a Prayer' wasn't too far behind.

Rene let me buy the next three rounds. She introduced me to her friends, and not a minute after handshakes did Rene pull me aside and tell me all about the venereal diseases her 'sluts' had contracted: Karol (Pollack, gap between her teeth – condyloma) and Moira (Irish, left-handed – Herpes Simplex Virus-2). I think it's safe to say that Rene wanted me all to herself.

'You're an *actor*?' she said, sips later. 'You gotta be kidding me, you're a fucking actor?'

'No. I'm a performer.'

'What's the difference?'

'If I could act I'd be an actor.'

'Funny guy!' she said, speaking into the mouth of her Woodpecker cider. 'I bet the girls just love that.'

'Every single one of 'em,' I laughed and put the Corona to my lips. 'I'm fuckin' hysterical!'

She dictated her phone number, and I entered the digits into my cell. She didn't have to repeat her name, but she did: 'I want to make sure you remember the pretty Italian chick you picked up at a wake.' And then seconds later: 'I don't like your goatee.'

'Well, fuck you, honey. I already got your number.'

'I guess I'm stuck with you then, huh?'

'We're practically married.'

The chorus to 'Livin' on a Prayer' came on, and everyone in the bar sang along, their wake-wear loosened with drink. I raised my fist in mock salute. When I turned to Rene, she was wiping her eyes with a paper napkin from the bar.

'It's okay,' she said, a curt laugh breaking through her reddened cheeks. 'I do this all the time.'

★

I don't normally play the straight man in scenes, and tonight is no different, having already put Winnie the Pooh through a spin cycle of withdrawal and intervention. Greg edits the scene and I recede to the backline. A little sweaty from the stage lights, I wait to support the next scene.

My mind drifts to the bandage on my chest and the

stitches inside my mouth – the traumatic evocations: Rene's scent on my t-shirt, her Irish boyfriend's bloody fist, Christopher Robin wearing Pooh's pelt.

These details, I like to think, would make for an interesting character. Someone you'd like to watch for a while. I try to tell myself that's the reason I stayed on for so long (nine months the lover). I try to chalk up the last nine months of my life to the performer in me – the ham who's always searching for hysteria and comedy – but that's too simple. I loved her.

I was wrapped up in her details. I loved her in parts: imperfections, peccadilloes, the word 'wish' tattooed on her ankle. Her name felt so good to say – still feels good – I felt like a poet pronouncing it.

Rene, I'm on the backline, for what feels like forever, *Rene*-ing to myself.

The audience quietens down.

We were always drunk, and she was always a bitch – I loved it.

'Your abs are disgusting,' she said one night, tracing my hard-earned four-pack with her fingertips. 'You should just stop working out and get a beer gut like Paul.' Then she peppered my stomach with kisses.

The first time we made love – after an afternoon stroll through Central Park ('You're really trying to make this romantic, aren't you?') and 60 ounces of Budweiser – she cried, something she 'always did'. At first I thought it was out of guilt, she having some poor mick bastard waiting for her at home, but then she kissed me so hard, caught my bottom lip between her teeth, and pulled me deep inside her, her legs wrapped so tight around my lower back that I couldn't move.

'Just stay inside of me!' she said, her face feverish. 'Just stay inside me.'

I kissed her cheeks as more tears slid out from the corners of her eyes, then cupped her ears, dampening my fingers with her sweat.

'Thank you,' I said. I buried my face between her neck and shoulder and wept. I wasn't on stage. *We* weren't on stage. We lay there until her legs slackened and her lips found my ear, then her tongue, her teeth –

She moaned, pulling my hair in order to get at my mouth, our tongues uncontrollable and sloppy. She made a motion, and then I was on my back, my head hanging over the edge of the bed. And she pushed and pushed – the red bed sheet slipping beneath us – until gravity yanked me to the floor and Rene went flying into the closet door. We were two thuds, drunken and naked on the cold hardwood. Rather than move to the bed, we lay there at the point of impact. She slid me neatly inside her again, and we remained motionless, examining each other: a pimple at her temple, the pads of her feet cool, a slight tinge of beer on her breath. Instead of saying, 'I love you' we laughed and kissed, until our laughter grew hysterical, until it hurt.

I come off the backline and Doug follows me. I want to

relive the event, every single event that brought Rene and me to our *first* ridiculous moment. I wish I could shoot Rene into Doug's brain, give him all of her sweet complexities, every little detail.

'Rene,' I start, inadvertently addressing the audience. 'You know, I was gonna wear that dress tonight. I'm glad I didn't though. That would've been so embarrassing.'

I'm ready to play it all over again, ready to leave out the extra *e* from her name, ready to take her to Central Park, ready to get drunk again – but of course, that's impossible. Rene's not on the stage with me – Doug is. And the cough in the crowd is another reminder of the impossibility.

'Yes, it would have been embarrassing, huh, Clara?' he responds, his voice and body attempting a feminine form. 'You know what else would be embarrassing? Huh? If you accidentally burned all of my dresses so I couldn't compete in the beauty pageant.'

'Rene, just one –'

Another cough.

'– more time, please.'

And then another. Doug waits.

I *know* I'm on stage, and there's nothing else for me to do but to take on the Valley-girl archetype and respond, 'Well, like…you know how clumsy I am with matches.'

'No more chances!' Doug responds. 'It's over!'

'I know it is.'

The scene painfully rolls on – prays for an edit. The audience has definitely laughed harder.

★

By the last month we'd become ridiculous. We pumped the stereo but didn't listen to it. Rene cried more, and so did I, and there we were, weeping pathetically until we were in bed. Barred and buried in our afternoons, we napped like the old and drank like alks, splurging on bottom-shelf spirits. She'd always 'have to leave' the Cocoon – that's what I called the apartment. She called it the Honeycomb, a place for her to sleep and get fat. And like a girlfriend, she put on weight. I accepted the extra pounds because they were hers. I kneaded her softened muscles, her cellulite – another detail to love, another part of her in need of whatever I could give her. But I was not her boyfriend. She never let me forget that.

Paul would always call, P A U L lighting up the monitor of her cell phone, his ringtone the chorus to U2's 'Sunday, Bloody Sunday'. I'd sing along, fist in the air, until she'd tell me to be quiet, that she'd 'have to pick up'. Her voice would change (become more girlish), and she'd use words like 'baby' and 'love' while I'd be nibbling for attention at her ankles. This always pissed her off.

I would try to piece Paul together, to make a man out of the few details that I knew about him: beer gut, Irish, calls all the time. From Rene's side of their phone conversations I learned that she loved him '*so much*'; she never hung up the phone without telling him. Even when they argued over rent (which happened a lot) she always let him know that he was loved. She never said she loved me, but there she was in my bed, in my arms. I never said, 'I love you', either, but I was there.

He liked U2 – the fucking guy was Irish, of course he did! – and Rene loved him. She loved him so much that she could not (would not) leave him. And I'd asked her a bunch of times, 'Why don't you leave him?' – not in *those* words – but I'd say, 'Just stay a little bit longer', which meant the same thing to me. And she'd always respond, as if singing a refrain, 'I can't, I can't, I can't…'

I grew weary of her exits and tried to make it harder for her to leave – 'Don't leave the Honeycomb, baby!' I'd say, playfully barring the door with my naked body and kisses, lifting her, then dropping her on the bed, hoping to screw her into a coma. But the sexual chloroform would never work, and she'd escape, one time saying, 'God, you're acting like you're in love or something!'

Bitch.

I grew jealous of Paul's ignorance – he never suspected a thing; even after the Halloween party. I bet he thought I was just some drunken asshole who'd gotten out of line. Fucking ridiculous! Who suggests *BREAKUP*!

Maybe none of it ever happened. Maybe Rene and I were just some improvised scene, some mutation of a suggestion from the back row. I know I'm not the only one onstage. But there's a scene in my head:

I *lie on my bed, denuded.* **RENE***, wearing nothing but my grey t-shirt, exposes her buttocks as she turns over/away from me. I run* *my hands along her body – even though we've just made love, and I should know that she's real, I'm still thinking of the possibilities. I decide to push it.*

ME (*in my best brogue, which sounds quite Scottish*): So, tell me about this guy. This guy you've been seeing. I know you have. I can see it in your eyes. Whenever you come home to me, you look like a new woman. A fair maiden, that's what you are. Aye! *I move her ponytail and kiss the back of her neck.* So, tell me, this lover of yours…does he fuck you proper? Do you come with him? Aye! *I move her hair again and kiss her ear.* Does he love you proper? Does he love you as much as I do?

RENE *cries like she always does, and I'm there to spoon with her, until she has to go.*

It's the last time she comes to the Honeycomb.

★

Dan and AJ roll around on the floor, and the audience comes alive again, their laughter almost sticky. Doug and Greg follow them downstage, and all four of them knock into the front row. Pretty soon they're growling and slowly clawing at the patrons' ankles, scratching the laughter out of their shins.

I'm lost on the backline.

★

The word 'wish' tattooed on her ankle. The last grey t-shirt of mine she wore. The way she chose her words: 'I don't want to see you ever again.'

Why didn't she just sing, 'I can't, I can't, I can't...'?

Two days without an R-E-N-E ring or vibration – I had to break the first rule! I had to run over to their apartment, bang on the door, force my way in no matter what the cost. I had to see where she slept when she wasn't sleeping with me. I had to see the alternative Honeycomb. I had to see this poor mick bastard she loved '*so much*' – I had to see if my impersonation was dead on.

He wasn't there. But the bedroom was. Rene was, standing in the living room, crying like she always did – even though there was no music playing, even though she was sober, even though the place stunk of *rettes* and laundry, even though it wasn't my place. Not my Cocoon!

'This is where you live? This your Honeycomb?' I said, looking over the plaid loveseat. 'Where do you sleep?'

'The bedroom's in there.'

It was all bed. All bed and Winnie the Pooh. Figurines, birthday cards, posters, clock, nightlight. Every wall. Every inch of the place. 'I'm obsessed,' she'd told me one day. 'You should see my bedroom.'

Yeah. I sat down on the bed, felt smothered by the cartoon bear. She came to the doorway naked: paunch, pubic hair thriving, calves relaxed. She pushed me back onto a company of stuffed Poohs, unbuckled-unzipped me, then pulled my jeans and drawers down to my knees. I was pinned.

'Let me stay inside you,' I said, trying to bridle her hips. 'I just want to stay inside you.'

She held my arms at my sides, bared her unstained teeth, bit down on her lower lip, and closed her eyes. I went – shook till exhaustion.

She let me pull up my pants, and then she led me to the door.

'I don't want to see you ever again.'

★

Whatever the guys' scene is, it reaches its apex, so I edit it. With our 25-minute set coming to a close we probably have room for just one more. I have a scene etched in my mind already; I initiated it about a week ago:

I stumble – drunk of course – into Donovan's Pub, Halloween night. Unable to find an adult-size costume, I was forced to buy a children's size (6-8 years old) Winnie the Pooh suit. I cut it up and fitted the pieces to my frame as best I could: leg warmers, sleeves that covered my forearms, Pooh's torso worn like a backpack, his head as a helmet. A yellow polo shirt and blue shorts cover what Pooh's pelt cannot.

I get wrapped up in some synthetic gossamer that's been draped across the entrance. Witches, nurses, angels, devils, mullet wigs, false crooked teeth, etc. take up most of the space in the pub. James's 'Laid' plays on the jukebox.

RENE, *hair pulled into a side ponytail, sips from a martini glass. She is surprised to see me.*

ME: What are *you* doing here?

RENE: What did you do to Pooh?

ME: I had to, Rene, I was freezing to death. I had to survive. (Pause) So, who are you supposed to be?

RENE: Deb from *Napoleon* –

ME: You know, I was gonna wear that. Would've been embarrassing, huh?

RENE: Please leave.

ME: You here alone?

RENE: Just leave, I don't want there to be any trouble.

ME: Then what's the point of me staying?

I stumble into her, grab hold of her ponytail, and kiss her hard and sloppy. Her martini glass falls to the floor. She tries to push me away, but I have her by the hair. She cries. *I'm struck on the back of the head; then I'm thrown into a wall. I look up at* **PAUL***, wearing his cheap costume. I've seen three others just like him already.*

ME: Fuck you, Napoleon Dynamite!

I charge, my open palm connecting on Rene's reddened face. I'm soon on the floor, being stomped, bottles breaking around and under me. I cover my face and crawl to the door. Paul's on my back, breaking his hand on my head. Napoleon Dynamite is beating the shit out of Winnie the Pooh! Fucking ridiculous! Breakup!

At some point, I'm free to run away. It's so cold outside. The blood in my moustache is drying. I check the slice in my shirt, the gash runs deep under my skin. I've lost my Pooh head.

'I feel like Christopher Robin's crawled up my asshole and ripped me from the inside out.'

The audience takes this in, as do the rest of The Baldwins. I'm by myself for what feels like forever.

Dan springs forward and justifies my line: 'Pooh's overdosing! C'mon, everyone!'

I fall to the floor and do the OD-shake. Dan cradles my head in his lap, pretending to weep. The other guys come off the backline to support:

Stay with us, Pooh!

You can't die!

Dreams don't die!

Where's the rent!

The audience is in hysterics. I convulse for the last time and play dead.

'He's gone,' Dan says. 'Just like Eeyore.'

Blackout.

Applause.

★

We bow and give thanks to the audience. There's some leftover Southern Comfort, which we offer to those who want it.

'That was *my* suggestion,' a white kid in a hooded sweatshirt says as he takes a Dixie cup. He downs the shot and leaves the room, happy with *Breakup*.

Really, he could've suggested anything and I would have thought of Rene. Try it. Pick a word, and try *not* to follow it back to your lover of nine months, try *not* to obsess over every detail, every traumatic, hysterical, *ridiculous* specific. The stuff that made your scenes.

Grainne

Gareth Storey

A little background to this story is that my ma and da split up and divorced when I was still playing with He-Man figures. I ate peanut butter and strawberry jam sandwiches for breakfast, lunch and dinner (when my ma let me). I was sent to Dublin hospital after an older kid with the same name as me, and who lived on my street, threw a brick that hit me on the left side of my head, and I had been in a coma for three days. The whole time I was in that hospital bed my da's favourite song 'Purple Rain' played in my head.

After this I moved to England. Out of the choices my ma chose Slough because my Uncle Johnny lived there and she wanted to get away from Ireland. Living with a single parent wasn't the greatest ride but I did get to do a lot of things that other kids didn't. I ate crisps and drank cans of coke for breakfast (my ma never woke up before me); I watched violent films like *Robocop*, *The Terminator*, *Predator* and *Aliens* when other kids at school couldn't; *and* as an only child on payday my ma would treat me to a Happy Meal at McDonald's (I just wanted the toy) then a film at the local cinema. We saw many films there in that old cinema with its two screens and dirty red carpet and I thought of it as a home away from home. This is where I developed my obsession with films and since those days I don't think a day has gone by without me watching at least one film. Apart from that time I stayed with my da and his new wife in County Wicklow, Ireland. They didn't have a video player in the house they rented – Jesus, they didn't even have a TV. It felt like a bad dream.

I was staying with my da for two weeks in this house, in the middle of nowhere without being able to watch films, which seemed pointless because I'd mostly packed my bag with videos my ma had bought for me: *Nico*, *Marked for Death* and *Kickboxer*. I swear I looked at the video covers every day, studying the pictures and imagining the scenes that happened before and after that particular picture. This helped me get through those two weeks where my da thought he could get me interested in flying a kite (what?), walking up mountains (no way), and reading books (boring). All I wanted to read were the synopses on the back of the video covers. That was until my da's friends came to stay for one night. They brought their daughter with them who was ten, a year older than me, and everything changed.

I didn't really play with girls much at school. It wasn't because I thought they smelled or they had some disease, it was because at my school boys and girls didn't play together. The boys – we either spent our time talking about toys, trainers and films or we played football. The girls – from what I could tell – played hopscotch and all of that, or stood around in divided groups: 1) Ugly girls, 2) Fat girls, 3) Skinny girls, 4) Popular girls (they were usually skinny and blonde), 5) Weird girls (these girls didn't speak or just smelled).

So here I was, desperate to do something in this nowhere land of Wicklow and the only hint towards having fun was playing with a girl. Her name was Grainne, she was skinny (maybe popular), she had shoulder-length brown hair and was wearing a red and white tartan dress. I wonder what she thought of me; I had a side parting (which I did myself) and was wearing a Ghostbusters t-shirt with Slimer on it, blue jeans and big Nike trainers. I had to have those Nike trainers because at school you were only as cool as your trainers: if you wore Nike or Reebok – you were cool; Gola or Hi-Tec – you were sad and no one cool would like you. So I guess we sized each other up as far as kids do, then we sat around in the living room while the adults talked. After half an hour of us sitting there without saying anything to each other, my da turned round from his chair and says to me: 'The two of you go on outside. John, show her the stream.'

The stream was crap, a little bit of clear water from the mountains running through some green grass. Wow! The beauty of Ireland!

We walked out of the house. There were no other houses near us – my da said our neighbours were three miles away. I didn't know what to say so I asked her did she like TV. Her green eyes lit up then and she started telling me about the cartoons and shows she watched. I liked most of what she liked apart from the crappy girly shows.

'Why isn't there a TV at your house?' she asked, like it was my fault.

My interest for her started growing with this question. She liked TV – we had a common interest. I looked at the stream, thinking of an answer.

'My da works in television and sees it all day and all night so this is his holiday away from it,' I replied.

She nodded and smiled. She believed me.

'I'm gonna be like my da when I grow up,' I said, 'but I'm not gonna work in TV. I'll be an actor like Arnie or Van Damme.'

The words that came out of my mouth were new to me. I had never thought these things before.

'Wow! Really?' she asked. 'How much do you like films?'

I answered straight away.

'Loads – I've seen *Gremlins* a 113 times. I even collected the cards. It's great! I write it down in my book whenever I watch a film so I don't lose count, and the other film I've watched the most is *Robocop*. I've seen it 98 times but that came out after *Gremlins* so that's why I haven't seen it as much.'

I thought with this kind of spiel from me she would run back up the hill to the house. I had no control over my

34

mouth when it came to films, but instead she smiled and looked at me. I felt unusual; I can't remember a girl before her looking at me that way.

We spent the afternoon messing around by the stream and talking until I asked her if she liked kites. She said she did, so we went back to the house and I asked my da if we could play with the kite because he seemed more interested in it than I did until now. He looked at me and laughed. I could see empty bottles of wine on the kitchen table and the rest of the adults were smoking. He took it from the shelf in the coat cupboard near the front door and said: 'Have fun, son.' He only called me son when he was drunk, or when he picked me up or dropped me off at the airport. But when he said it I felt more like his son than I usually did.

We took the kite down the hill to the stream then walked up another hill. It was windy and looked like it would rain but it didn't rain until about an hour after – when we were at home and bored by the kite already. Grainne was great with the kite and I had way more fun with her than with my da. She looked happy controlling this thing flying in the air and always laughed when the kite crashed to the ground, unlike me or my da. When it happened with us I had to run and pick it up and be careful not to get it tangled up. With her I didn't mind, I liked running to pick it up.

We got back to the house and the rain poured. The sky that was a bright blue most of the day had now turned a dull grey. I was glad to be inside. We ate dinner with the adults who were still drinking wine and smoking. They were listening to a band called Talking Heads which I thought was a cool name. After dinner Grainne and I went to my room so I could show her my video cases. She hadn't seen *Nico* or *Marked for Death*, my Steven Segal films or *The Terminator*. I wanted her to see them. I wanted to know if she would like them as much as I did. I told her to ask her parents if they would rent or buy them for her when she got back to Dublin and she said she would.

We played board games that were left in the house by someone else until around ten thirty when my da's wife came into my room and said we had to go to bed. There were two beds in my room and she said that Grainne would sleep in the spare one. We were told to go straight to sleep. She closed the door.

We were both excited. We had become good friends throughout the day and we were happy to have met each other. We brushed our teeth together and then jumped into our separate beds. In the dark we talked in whispers. Grainne said she wanted to move her bed closer to mine so I got out of my bed and she got out of hers and we pushed the beds together. We were quiet because no one came in to check on us. I had never kissed a girl but I could sense it was coming. I reached my hand over to her bed and asked her to hold my hand. She did. Then she moved closer to me. I could smell her breath. She smelt of garlic and mint toothpaste and I'm sure I did as well – we had both eaten the same dinner and both brushed our teeth. We held hands and talked. I had no idea about love or sex. I was a naïve child of divorce on holiday in Wicklow. I told her I really liked her and she said the same to me. Our bodies met together and we kissed using tongues, we didn't touch each other though we kept holding hands. I wanted to tell her that I loved her. I wanted her to stay or for me to go with her when she left for Dublin. I didn't want to be left alone in this house for another week.

I asked her to wake me up before she left but when I woke up she was gone. I started crying and sat in my pyjamas in the moved-together beds. I pushed them apart and opened the curtains. It looked like it would rain. I counted the days I had left with my da before I was pushed on to one of my nanas and the tears kept coming. I missed my ma, I missed watching videos, I missed Grainne.

Fucked

Katharine Coldiron

'Whaddya say?' One and a half of the sweetest words in the English language. We stand there, and I breathe in and out, and he looks at me with oh-God-those-eyes, and I raise my skirt even higher and lean against the wall, fiery. One leg up, one foot on tiptoe, and sensation, that's all I am for another ten minutes. How does it end? How *should* it end?

★

I knew this guy had a temper as soon as he laughed at one of my jokes. The smile was too easy. Any guy who can smile so fast, teeth slipping out like knives, has definitely got the same kind of quickness to his temper and that's just not a good thing. We were in a noisy bar a few weeks ago and I shouted, 'Nice place for meditation, right?' He laughed, and I saw that easy smile, and I thought ohhh, I'm all in, dealer. It wasn't even an hour later that he was pounding me against his mattress and I was thinking about Charlie.

The dates went by and I didn't see the temper, but I was ready for it.

★

'I want you,' I whisper. 'Oh, please don't move an inch...'

★

So this doesn't surprise me much, that he's decided to freak out over a little thing like a lost garage ticket. Yeah, it's $20, but either of us could afford it and we were at the club almost long enough for that anyway, at the hourly rate. I'm watching him punch the wall, and I'm really tired. My calves hurt from my stilettos, my head aches, and this is so stupid.

My mother's voice comes into my head, suddenly, telling me to walk away from this. *You deserve better. Think of your father.* My father, right. She used to say that to remind me about the mistakes she'd made, not to shame me. I never knew my dad, and I'm not sure she even remembers his name. Some shrink books say that means that if I have the kid, and decide not to tell it who its dad is, or let him even know or care, I have some kind of self-approval for it because that's the way I was raised.

I remember Mom swatting me away from the stove, or other dangerous places, yelling 'What are you, stupid?' But I'm not stupid. Just fucked.

★

'You like that?' he mutters, with that greasy I'm-getting-laid undertone in his voice, and starts to move his hips more, because he's feeling like Shaft, because I'm moaning in his ear.

★

I tried to stay away from the stove even after I got older, but danger always beckons me. I have a respectable job and a respectable apartment, and I still go to places like the Down Under Bar (not named for the Outback) and meet guys like this. It's because I do these things, because I'm fucked, that I end up in situations like this, standing here with a cigarette in my hand (shouldn't smoke, I think, but I can't let on), watching him punch the wall next to the recycling dumpster and wishing I was just at home with a James Patterson novel and maybe, like, a Meg Ryan movie. I hate chick flicks, usually, but here I am with a guy who's punching the goddamn wall.

He's never hit me. I've never dated a man who hit me. That's a stove that even I can see is too hot without touching it. Still, somehow I was almost waiting for it from this guy. I could just see a black eye spreading bruisy fingers across my cheekbone because I talked back to him. I didn't know why I was with him, because I could always run back to Charlie, but Charlie cared about me, Charlie was nice, Charlie's apartment had vintage Dylan posters on the walls. This guy here, punching the wall, was exciting. Right?

I knew that we couldn't stay there forever with him yelling about the stupid ticket, and besides I was bored. So I did what I had to do, you know – I used what I've got to relax him. When he took a minute to rub his knuckles in hard-breathing silence, I passed my hand across his shoulder and drew near him. Murmuring some bullshit to him about calming down, it's so much better if you just relax, baby, I started kissing his neck and running my hands over him. He, like a child, stubbornly refused at first to be interested, but then I felt his hands on my ass and I knew I was starting to win.

★

'Yes,' I say, my breath quickening. 'Yesssssss.'

★

The only time I ever felt like I wasn't getting cheated out of sex was with Charlie. Charlie wasn't one of those guys I met – picked up – at a bar. He saw me in a coffee shop and made a joke about soy milk, and at first I still hit the bars after he dropped me off at home. Took him months to tell me he wanted to have sex.

But I couldn't hang on to it. I realised he cared for me on that last night, and I was too afraid. We were doing it, and I started to think, so very hard, about how many pills I had accidentally skipped that week, and I started getting panicked and shaking, and Charlie was getting near the finish line, and I told him to stop, and I was crying over and over, I don't want to have a baby, I don't want to have a baby. He stopped. I couldn't believe it, but he stopped.

The next night I went to the Down Under and I picked up Mr Wall-Puncher. That was rough and tough and good stuff, and in my head I was screaming for Charlie the entire time.

But if Charlie had found something wrong with me, years down the line, I'd be on my ass all over again, and it wouldn't be my doing. That'd hurt. The phone call from Charlie the next week hurt like that: he told me he understood what I was like (I'm fucked, I know it), but that he wanted me to come back to him if something changed. I believed him, but it was too damned simple to stay with him, he was too perfect.

This guy's easy. He's not Charlie; he'd never stop if I told him I was worried about a baby. A baby would be my problem, and so it is. Still, it's easier to be with someone who can't hurt you. When they say no thanks, you just shrug your shoulders and move on to the next in line.

So here I am and we're starting to really make out now, and he's moving me into the corner between the two walls, which I suppose was what I wanted in the first place but now that it's happening I'm upset at him for being so crude. He pushes me against the wall and I'm really stuck now, really pushed into doing this thing, next to a recycling bin. And if this were Charlie we'd be smiling wickedly at each other and I'd blush whenever I thought of it, but it's not Charlie.

★

'Oh God,' he starts to say, breathing like a horse. 'Oh Jesus God.'

But then everything flips, like it usually does, and I stop thinking about how this guy's about to fuck me and I start thinking about how I'm about to have sex with this guy, and that even though it's him it's still sex in a public place. One more story to tell my friends. They seem to like hearing about this shit.

Maybe all of this does have something to do with my father, whoever he was. Trying to fill up that hole. Not that I believe in Freud so much, but that him not existing for me left a gap. I don't want to fuck my dad, but I want to fuck to fill up the hole. My own hole, I guess, it's all one big hole to men.

Charlie was the only one who didn't seem interested in my body, but my*self*. He wanted to hear about how I felt. He wanted to talk for hours in his bed, sheets puddled around us. I think he wanted to look at me and talk to me as much as he wanted to grope and fuck me. If he even wanted to do those things. Sometimes I thought he didn't, but avoiding them would have conflicted with what sex is, mechanically. I don't know, it's really strange, I mean all men are the same, right? They're all gropers and fuckers at the core. Charlie might not have seemed like one but he probably was. My father. A long line, these years of men in dark beds with neon flashing against the sheets. And I'm against this wall, and my skirt is starting to be indiscreetly high around my hips.

It's funny that even with the baby I want this. I don't know if it's Charlie's or his, and I know that either way it's not going to matter. Charlie won't want it. No man wants a baby like this, with someone like me. But I feel weird, like I have a secret that has to do with the secret we're about to share when he gets his dick out of his pants. And it has something to do with sex, but the way men understand it, there's some kind of locker-room connection between having sex and a baby (like the locker-room connection between sex and love), and the way we understand it is somehow different.

But I don't know. This secret here, between my legs, is the only one he's interested in for the time being. And I'm starting to get interested too, even though thoughts of Charlie keep interrupting me.

*

He slows down briefly. 'Are you still on the pill?' he says. I am so wrapped up in it that I mutter 'Doesn't matter' before I even think about it. This still doesn't stop him, but his motion gets somehow distracted. 'What do you mean?' he breathes, panting a little. I know that I have made a catastrophic error but I feel so *good*, the anonymity and the spontaneity of the situation are starting to catch on to my pleasure centres, and I say, I say, 'I'm pregnant.'

He stops cold.

★

But God, I didn't know *this* would happen. I thought that before it came to this I'd get beyond myself somehow, get beyond the hole I had to fill up, learn to live, even if I had to live with this child that I wasn't sure I wanted.

★

'You're *what?*' he shouts, right into my ear. He pulls back and looks at me, not stunned but fucking angry. I start to get scared, a little, and I say it again. 'I don't know if it's yours, it might still be Charlie's but –'

WHAP.

He's done it. He hit me. And then he starts fucking me again, but this time it's not about excitement and not about garages, it's about fucking me. 'I can't believe you. I can't believe you! How could you be so irresponsible?'

Now this was really not fair because he had sex with me twice before he even knew I was on the pill. I start to say something but he grabs my face with one hand while he's fumbling around in his back pockets somewhere with the other hand. I see red rage in oh-God-those-eyes, and I'm suddenly really, really cold.

★

My mother tried to tell me to find a nice boy, but she didn't explain how she'd failed at it. When I was little I dreamed about princes who would caress my face, knights who would kiss me on the forehead. I never had a boyfriend like that until Charlie – they all just wanted what was in my panties. After a few years I started to wonder more about my father, and wonder if my mom had marched in and out of bedrooms until she had me, just like I was doing now. Was it genetic?

I shouldn't have gone back to the hot stove at the Down Under that night. It burned to have sex with someone else. I should have called Charlie back after the message he left on my voicemail, the one about understanding, and 'come on back when you need to'. I was thinking too much about the baby, because I'd started to wonder about it already, and I thought that would run Charlie right out of my life. But I'm starting to realise that he actually would have wanted this baby, because…because he actually would have wanted it with me.

*

From behind his back he gets a switchblade. Really. I'm standing there being fucked, still, and I'm looking at this knife, and I'm thinking, oh, come on, this isn't really happening, someone come and tell me I've been Punk'd. But my insides seem to know that's not going to happen, and I'm starting to feel like I'm going to throw up.

But there's no time for that, because what happens is he comes, explosively, and yells out, and slices me open across the line of my pelvis below my belly button. Blood pours out onto his jeans and drips down my skirt, and all I can feel is a flaring whiplash of pain somewhere below my waist. He pulls out of me, zips up his fly, and stands over me, because of course I've fallen down. He puts his face close to mine with the knife between them and says, 'Wanna lose the baby?' 'No,' I whisper. Maybe he's struck by the awfulness of what he's just done, or maybe he sees that I'm a person, or maybe he's just tired of the whole thing, because he walks away.

★

I guess the only thing you can do to stay sane in a situation like this is not to think about how you got there. I don't believe that women should be punished for the bad things they do, but I do believe that there are things I should have done not to end up like this, so I'm not going to think about them. I'm not going to think about how I could have listened better to what my mother told me (and what she didn't tell me). I'm going to think about how to get out of this one, because it's really not so different from what's been happening all along. By knife or by cock, it comes to the same thing a lot of the time. It's hate that keeps them running to the next one and the next one, and it's hate turned inward that keeps *you* running to them.

Most of them, anyway. Some of them really value what happens when it happens. And it's somehow not an invasion all of a sudden, because they recognise what it is they're doing to you, and that means that they're not doing it *to* you anymore.

Mostly I'm going to think about Charlie, and what he will do to this guy when he finds out what he did to me. At least I hope he will do those things. Most of all, I hope that my baby and me will be there to see them.

The Chief Remedies

The Grief Benches

Chelsey Flood

I pass the Grief Benches on my way to work. No one is on them today. Last night I saw a couple there, him wet eyed and her with her head down. She scrunched her eyes tight as I passed and I remember thinking she was a fraud. It's alright if you don't want to cry, I thought, there's no point pretending for my benefit.

Me and Jack christened the benches when we were walking home from work half drunk. Three benches on a slanted grassy verge with nothing nearby, facing out to sea, a kind of limbo: perfect for grieving. I look at them whenever I pass and wonder what it is about grief that makes people want to get out of their houses.

All day at work 'Too Much Too Young' by the Specials keeps going round my head. Me and Jack heard it as we came out of Boots, after we had spent our last five pounds on a pregnancy test. It made us laugh, hearing it then, it was like we had our own soundtrack.

Keep a generation – gap. Start. Wearing. A. Cap.

Now it goes round and round inside my head, followed by that drum beat, which starts to sound more and more like circus music. It still makes me laugh, but it's a different kind of laughter now, not very close to humour at all. Jack texts me to see how the test went and I can't bring myself to text back.

When the Wizened Man shuffles into work, the song disappears. I'm not going to hurt you, he says to my boss and she smiles at him in a way that makes it clear she doesn't think he could.

His skin looks hard all over, like cured meat, like the life has been sucked out of him. Like the head of a garlic prawn. As he asks Megan for a drink he looks so hopeful that I don't know how she can resist. He glances at me, and I look away quickly, but not before Megan notices.

At our last meeting, she said she thought I'd been encouraging the tramps of the town. She told me not to speak to them anymore while I was working. We need to observe a zero tolerance rule towards them. They must realise they cannot get alcohol from this restaurant. I just nodded, not really knowing what to say to someone who thought that this was what needed to happen.

Jack loved it when he heard. It was his favourite story for weeks. He even made it into a toast.

He'd say: Here's to zero tolerance!

And I'd say: And here's to homelessness!

It didn't make any sense, but it made us feel original, and it made us laugh.

I'm not a bad person you know, the Wizened Man is saying to Megan. His eyebrows lift earnestly, dragging the wrinkled face below up and over the old, old bones underneath. Megan lifts a manicured hand to her nose, as if she's smelling herself to keep him out.

I just drink too much, he tells her, I drink too much vodka, but I'd never hurt you. I just want a little bit of vodka. He goes as if to move towards her, lifts one foot, but then thinks better of it and places his foot back down.

Megan takes this as her cue, and raises her voice slightly, tells the Wizened Man he has to leave *now*.

I can't stay out of it any longer. I put my hand on his coarse, fisherman's jumper and link my arm through his, imagining he's a well-turned-out old gent in an expensive hotel lobby.

Allow me to escort you to the door, sir, I say, hoping he's imagining the same thing and that my manoeuvre seems vaguely elegant.

Megan stays by the bar, aghast.

I just wanted to apologise to you two young ladies, he says to me on the way out and the sweet, fermented stink of alcohol fills my nostrils. I smile at him graciously like a well-trained hotel porter, discreetly letting go of his grubby elbow when we're on the pavement.

As he tells me about his broken arm and the lads that did it, I try to listen, but I can't concentrate. I'm trying to understand that there's a foetus growing inside me, that this foetus could actually become a person living in the world.

The Wizened Man's dry lizard lips are moving, saying things I've heard a thousand times before, and I'm just thinking what chance has he got?

I think about him, just born, somebody's baby. I think about Megan, believing that saving money is more important than giving a thirsty man a little shot of vodka and I feel sad for her, like she's fallen for a terrible trick. And then I feel sad for myself because I know she's not the only one.

I look past the Wizened Man's head with his dry lips still moving and imagine all the people rushing by us are children. Their faces lift, become more expectant, like they're waiting to see what will happen next.

I look back at the Wizened Man, trying to see the bemusement in his eyes as wonder at the beauty of the world rather than surprise at its cruelty. But it's impossible. As he peers at me, holding the left arm that no longer hangs properly with his filthy right hand, the magic is broken and the people in the street are the same aging, distracted adults they always were.

I have to go back inside then, to get out of the way of the people on the street, to leave the Wizened Man behind. And I can't bear the way he hovers by the doorway, saying goodbye louder and louder like he wants to carry on a conversation that we weren't even really having.

Megan shakes her head at me and tuts, opens her lipsticked mouth to say something but I walk straight past her to the toilets, lock the door. I grimace ferociously in the mirror, gnash my teeth at myself but I don't feel any better.

When he gets home, Jack asks me what I want to do about the baby and I tell him not to call it that.

He tells me he doesn't want me to have an abortion, and I tell him I don't want to give birth.

It soon becomes clear that the decision is down to me, whether we like it or not.

I tell Jack he just wants me to have it so he knows what he's doing with his life and he doesn't deny it.

It would still be amazing, he says, putting his hand on my stomach.

It wouldn't always be a baby, I tell him, moving his hand away and standing up.

You don't have to do this by yourself, he says as I walk away, and I tell him to be quiet because it feels like everything we say is scripted.

And because what he's saying isn't true.

That night, when he curls his long, warm body around me, I imagine us as two foetuses under a quilt. I turn onto my back, spread my arms in the most unfoetal way I can.

When I fall to sleep I dream about a lost kitten.

I know it's officially autumn when I get to work, because Tony who sleeps in the kebab shop doorway is sitting at the bar.

'Ello darlin'! he exclaims as soon as he sees me, showing me his gums. I'm here for my autumnal coffee, he tells me, it's the end of British Summer Time.

I walk behind the bar to put a shot of coffee in the machine and Megan looks at me as if Tony's existence is my fault.

I'm going to do the banking, she says and we both ignore her.

If I'd known you were going to be here, I'd have put my teeth in, Tony says.

If I'd known you were coming I'd have worn a shorter skirt, I say back.

Tony puts his head back and laughs, his big phlegmy laugh cracking out around the empty restaurant. I put his coffee down and pour a slug of whiskey in it, happily reducing Megan's profits.

Well, I've been living in this place for six and a half years today, he starts and I raise my eyebrows as if it's the first time I've heard him say this.

Six and a half years. You didn't work here back then, did you?

No, I tell him, I was still at college.

And how old were you then? he asks me.

I tell him I was eighteen.

Really? he asks in a soft, surprised voice. He pauses for a minute then, fleshy eyelids threatening to fall down onto watery eyes as he stares down at brown, speckled hands. I imagine those hands as they might have been once, soft and pink as an infant's, or hard and calloused as a working man's.

Eighteen, eh? And where have those years gone? he asks me gently.

I shrug and he takes a sip of his coffee, silent for once.

He clears his throat elaborately, then starts telling me about his girlfriends when he was my age: Pauline with the long legs and Dorothy who used to give him blowies in the back of his Morris Minor.

I put some more whiskey in his mug and offer him a slice of carrot cake.

You're too good to me, he says.

As I smile back at him, I realise I'm being kinder to this stranger than I have been to Jack for weeks. And I don't even know why. I think about the warm body that I left in bed this morning, the way his hair works itself into a tangle where he has been sleeping on it, and the creased look his face gets from lying on his front, then I look at Tony, staring into his coffee, frail strands of hair just about clinging to his head, and I wonder at myself.

I take my bag into the kitchen and steal two sirloin steaks for tea.

On the way home, I see a lone woman on the central Grief Bench, her wispy blonde hair catching in the cold wind. The sky above her is low and dark, and so is the sea she stares blindly into. I speed up, fumbling in my bag for my keys.

I start preparing tea straight away, trying to remove the woman's blank face with routine and domesticity. But instead, I just imagine her kitchen, empty. Her dead husband's shoes waiting by the door.

The steak seems different now, not food, just a stolen slab of flesh. I cook it anyway, trying not to think of morgues or sucked-out foetuses.

When Jack gets home I hug him hard and present him with his meal, then get him a beer, feeling slightly self-conscious about my fussing. He's unnerved and keeps looking at me in a way that makes me feel twitchy and unhinged.

I try not to be disgusted by the blood on our plates. But as he stuffs large chunks of steak into his mouth, I find myself becoming annoyed that he hasn't noticed I'm not eating mine.

Don't you want that? he says finally, when the steak's the only thing left on my plate. I tell him I've gone off meat and he just frowns, then sticks his knife into the middle of it, lifts it off my plate like some kind of Neanderthal.

That evening, Jack's sister Holly comes round. She's just got back from a year working in Southern Africa. She tells us about the state of things over there, then goes on and on about how weird it is to be watching *Eastenders*.

Jack tells her that I've been banned from conversing with the homeless and I wonder if he's doing it to please me, or because he thinks it will make us look more philanthropic. I laugh along anyway, looking amused then modest as necessary.

You know what she's like, he says in that proud voice. She nearly cried the other day about this old man we saw – she wanted me to give him my shoes!

I smile, like I always do when he says this kind of thing, but I'm wondering now whose benefit he's saying it for. If he's actually just saying it for me, to remind me how kind I am.

As Holly laughs, Jack pulls me close and just before I disappear into his shoulder I see Holly's face change. Her laugh falls into a slightly sad, slightly awkward smile and she looks towards the telly.

I stop going over everything in my head for a minute and try to see what she's seeing. I realise we look happy, with our dirty plates on the table and our clean clothes on the radiators. I think of Jack pulling me towards him like that and for a second I can see things as if I am him. I can imagine us muddling on together in this rented flat, with a little person that we've made by ourselves. And even though I know the picture isn't real, I realise what it means that he can see it. I kiss him hard on the mouth even though Holly's sitting right there, then I start asking her questions and listening intently to her answers. I give her my full attention, feeling ludicrously affectionate towards her.

The doctor confirms the test and I start to feel sick all the time.

Jack gets used to the idea that our lives aren't about to radically change and I get sacked for misconduct from the Quayside. It feels like the end of an era, like the end of school or the start of puberty or something. I start looking for a job where I won't get sacked for trying to help people, and go regularly to the doctors to be probed and examined. The day of the operation gets closer.

The night before I'm due to go into hospital Jack wakes me up, and I tell him to be careful of the kitten.

What kitten? he asks and I shake my head, confused.

I can't sleep, he says. Come for a walk with me.

The way he says it is enough for me to drag myself out of bed.

Outside the moon is bright and there are streaks of silver blue cloud high in the sky. The yachts on the water look gothic. Water slaps eerily against them every now and then.

It's obvious where we're both heading and we make our way to the Grief Benches without saying any words, but when Jack puts a foot on the step, I pull him back.

Let's sit here, I say, lifting myself up onto the wall instead. The damp moss seeps through my jeans but I don't care.

Jack puts his arm around me so I'm wrapped up in his coat and we both stare out to sea, dry eyed.

What Am I Doing Here?

Christine Cooper

Cerys stared at the screen in front of her. She had been waiting three minutes for her emails to load. Last week it had taken more than six. She had long since given up being in a hurry round here, even if she was paying by the minute; it just wasn't worth the stress. At the next computer but one, Emily had managed to access her mail with surprising speed, and was typing away. They usually managed the trip into town to check emails once a week; Cerys was never sure whether it was a treat or a chore.

Outside, the dusty South African sun beat down its forty degrees. Inside wasn't much better: a creaking fan made sluggish currents in the sticky air, and flies buzzed round Cerys's head. She looked at her watch. She'd been waiting almost five minutes. They'd have to get a move on to be back before the daily storm turned Soweto's streets to rivers. The rain came punctually at four o'clock every afternoon in summer. And it was serious rain: the sky would turn black, and release such a torrent of water that you might well be standing under a waterfall. Shop-owners locked up, market traders threw tarpaulin over their wares and ran for cover. There would be thunder and lightning too; beautiful, dramatic forked lightning. Then, after exactly twenty minutes, the storm would leave as suddenly as it arrived, and after another hour of that sun, there would be little evidence it had ever happened at all. Nothing happens by halves here, Cerys thought. And then she noticed that her emails had loaded.

Twenty-one new messages. She noticed four from her sister Nicola, one after the other, a neat patch of order amid the chaotic mailing lists and porn adverts, with the words *[No subject]* alongside each. The first was sent three days ago, then two days ago, and the final two yesterday. Cerys stared at them, and felt a strange tightening in her stomach. She clicked the first one, and the geriatric computer began to whirr.

★

That morning, Cerys and Emily had woken as usual to the sound of cocks crowing. There were always chickens running around in Soweto. It was never clear who owned them; they seemed to run around wild, living off what crumbs they could scratch out of the dust. The sun was barely up as the girls washed in last night's leftover water.

Once they had arrived at the orphanage, the girls got the older kids up and helped feed them their cornmeal breakfast. Most kids came to the orphanage as babies, abandoned by parents who couldn't afford them. Many were mentally or physically disabled and needed a lot of attention. The healthy ones were often fostered out, and didn't stay more than a couple of months. There were a lot more kids of all ages lately, AIDS orphans. Only this morning, a little girl of about two had been brought by a family friend, directed to the orphanage by the police. She was terrified, sobbing and clinging at the skirts of the woman who brought her. Cerys had to hold her as the woman left, and it made her heart break, as it always did. Sometimes she felt desperate to get out, away from the hardship and the heartbreak. But at other times she thought, how can I ever leave? How can I leave these children?

★

Message sent: 12/07/06 19:06

Mum and Dad asked me to write and tell you Granny fell over and broke her hip today. She's in the Heath and she's in a lot of pain. She'll be operated on tonight or tomorrow morning. We tried to ring you, but no answer. Will try again tomorrow.

Love Nic

★

Cerys grew up in small-town South Wales, in an ashamedly middle-class family. Her one saving grace was that her doctor parents had sent her to the local comprehensive. Cerys enjoyed being righteous, and she felt her class background did not allow her much opportunity for this.

She had quietly earned top grades all through school, and gone on to study History at university. She loved it – she attended conferences on the Iraq war and climate change, and joined the campaign to free Tibet. She was filled with theories, ideas and news stories to the point of overflowing. But the more she studied the past, the more she realised it was the present and the future that needed worrying about. The state of the world preyed on Cerys's mind, and she felt confined, fidgety. So after two years she dropped out and got on a plane to Johannesburg, with no idea what she would do there except that it would be something *useful*. Her parents were disappointed, she knew, but supportive. Well, financially supportive, at least. Every time she spoke to her mum on the phone, her mum would say: 'Did you hear about that English girl who was murdered in…? She was volunteering like you…'

★

Cerys had met Emily on her first night in South Africa, in the youth hostel they were both staying in, and had liked her instantly. Emily was straightforward with a down-to-earth northern accent. Cerys had lost count of the times Emily made her laugh after a bad day. She was older than Cerys and she knew about the orphanage from someone back in Manchester. After hearing about it, Cerys decided immediately to join her as a volunteer there.

For their first trip into Soweto, the girls had taken a taxi. The driver had not been happy about their destination, and in hindsight, it probably just drew more attention to them. But Cerys was sure they would never have found the orphanage on their own; Soweto was home to more than a million people. For the most part, it was laid out in a regimented grid structure; one dusty street lined with concrete-box houses was all but identical to the next. The houses were small and basic, with two tiny windows; the sort of thing that might be used to store logs or bikes in Britain. Corrugated iron roofing made them unbearably hot in summer, and cold in winter. A woman selling meat on a street corner waved her hand over her wares, and a cloud of black flies momentarily rose into the air before settling back to its meal. It was so hot that the middle-distance shimmered like a reflection in a lake, so that nothing seemed real.

The orphanage was a long concrete building, two storeys high. Inside, the walls were whitewashed but the floors were grey and bare. A more loveless-looking place she couldn't imagine. The director of the orphanage, an elegant but tired-looking woman in her forties, welcomed them.

'Come in, come in. I'm Jessica. Have some tea.'

The girls were waved into an office lit by a single bulb, and given tea so strong it could have been used as wood-stain. Soon they were meeting the kids in the playroom, and surrounded by little heads, excitedly bobbing and shouting, 'Hello! Hello!' It was all the English most of them knew. Donated toys lay on the floor and Cerys noticed that many were broken. She reached out and touched a little boy's coarse, springy hair.

'That's Terrence,' said Jessica. 'He was one of the first babies we looked after. He's been rather unlucky with foster-homes, poor darling,' she smiled. 'Come and see the baby room.' Some of the kids tried to follow them, but Jessica shooed them back in, speaking in rapid-fire Zulu.

The baby room contained rows of iron cots, each with a clip-chart on the end. Two women moved between the cots, picking up a baby here, feeding one there.

'It can be a struggle in here,' Jessica explained. 'Babies move in and out all the time. When we're full, it's hard to give enough attention to them all; to notice if they're sick, comfort them if they cry. We're desperately understaffed, but we just can't afford any more workers.'

Cerys loved it already.

*

Message sent: 13/07/06 14:37

Granny had a massive stroke on the operating table, and is basically in a coma. There's a machine helping her breathe. She can't move at all, and doesn't know if you talk to her. It's horrible.

Nic

★

Cerys's granny had lived in the house at the edge of the village forever, or that's how it seemed to Cerys. Her granddad died when she was very small, so the house had always been Granny's House. It was more than a hundred years old, and so had been infinitely more exciting than Cerys's parents' new build. Looking back, Cerys wasn't sure if it was the quantity of nooks and crannies suitable for hide-and-seek, or just that they got away with more at Granny's that made it so appealing. Then there were the delicious trays of cakes and puddings Granny pulled out of the Rayburn every visit. In spring, the field behind the house brimmed with daisies, and Cerys and Nicola would lie on their fronts in the long grass, ants tickling their bare legs, making daisy chains for Granny. Granny always put them on in delight, or draped them over a picture on the wall.

There was an old apple tree in the corner of the field. Its gnarled trunk had grown at a wind-twisted slant, making it perfect for climbing. They had regular climbing competitions, which their older brother Mike always won of course. But Cerys's favourite thing of all about Granny's house was the grandfather clock. It stood tall and regal in the baize-green hallway, dividing time neatly into small slices of silence with its commanding *tick, tick, tick*. The clock was always Cerys's special job when they helped Granny polish. She loved to turn the little key and open the secret door, to spy on the slow-swinging pendulum. It

chimed every fifteen minutes, day and night, soothing in
its regularity.

★

Message sent: 14/07/06 17:10

Just to say there's no change here. We try to arrange it so
someone is always with Granny. Mike's come down from
Birmingham. When I held Granny's hand, her eyelids
flickered. Tried to phone you again.

Nic

★

Cerys loved the orphanage, and hated it. After six
months it seemed like she'd never known any other life
but this; Emily was like her life partner, the children at
the orphanage became their extended family, and the
staff their drinking partners. They began to pick up
some Zulu.

One night, the girls had been at a party in their
neighbourhood. *Kwaito* pumped out of a cramped
concrete room, the bass turned up too loud for the ancient
speakers so it crackled at the edges. Revellers spilled out
into the street, and the stench of sweat hit the back of
Cerys's throat as she pushed her way in. Someone passed
her a bottle of rancid-tasting firewater, and then she was
dancing, twisting among the tightly packed bodies. The

crowd moved as one heartbeat to the music. Then there was a man, a beautiful man with fine dreadlocks hanging around his jaw. She felt his hands on her, and she *knew* that it was just the same as all the other times; that it was cool to dance with the white girl, cooler to sleep with her, and even cooler to marry her and get a ticket out. But still she leant into him and smiled.

Her arms around his waist, she felt something cold and hard behind him, pushed down the back of his jeans. Suddenly there was a gun in her hand. She thrust it back at him and backed off. His white teeth and the whites of his eyes smiled down at her. Scanning the crowd for Emily, she noticed almost all the guys had dark objects tucked into their belts. Cerys wasn't naïve (though certain relatives disagreed); this was no South Wales market town and she'd seen people carrying guns before. But she had never seen so many, and had never, ever held one.

Emily appeared at her shoulder and pushed a chipped tin cup into her hand.

Next thing Cerys knew, it was seven a.m. and Emily was shaking her awake. She felt wretched. But half an hour later, there she was in the older kids' dorm, just about managing to stay upright. Blessing, a boy of about six, had diarrhoea, and had pooed his bed. He was crying, and snot and tears made trails down his face. Cerys lifted him out and stripped his dirty clothes off. The smell made her retch. Then Blessing reached forward and put his two hands on his bed, hanging his head between them and sticking his bum out. A stream of projectile shit fired across the room and hit the far wall, where it made an impressive splat-mark. Cerys and Emily exchanged glances, and dissolved into giggles. Cerys tried to stifle her laughter – Blessing was a good kid, he really was – but she was helpless, and soon her face was as tear-streaked as his.

'Stop it, I can't laugh, I'll be sick…' she gasped.

Blessing cried and cried.

★

Message sent: 14/07/06 21:32

Granny died at 7.30pm. Mum and Mike were with her. Dad's really upset.

Nic

★

Cerys sat back in her chair, sweat dripping down her neck. She felt numb. She had known from the first email what the ending would be, but still she had forced herself to open each one in turn. Now that it was confirmed, she couldn't feel anything at all. There was just a queer…emptiness. She couldn't imagine Granny lying cold and dead in a hospital bed. That whole world was so far away. She opened her mouth to speak.

'My granny died,' she said, matter-of-factly. But it was as though someone else was saying it, and she didn't believe the words.

'What? Oh, no! I'm sorry!' Emily turned to her immediately. There was a pause. 'How...did she die?'

'She fell...had a stroke...Are you nearly ready to go? It'll rain soon.'

'Yes, yes, two minutes...'

The girls paid up and walked out into the daylight, where everything was whitewashed in the glare. Cerys put up her hand to shield her eyes. The sound of *kwaito* came from speakers a few doors down. Minibuses swerved in the road. A street-trader haggled with a customer. Emily waved down a number 67 and they jumped on, the vehicle picking up speed before Cerys's back foot was even in the door. The door was broken and someone in front of her was hanging on to it in an attempt to make it at least look shut. She passed a ten-rand note to the front passenger, who didn't give her any change. She was annoyed suddenly.

'Hey! Change?...Watch where you're going!'

The driver, in craning his neck to look at her, had almost hit a pedestrian.

'No change. You have to wait for someone else to get on.'

How hard could it be to have a float? Or fix the door? Or keep your eyes on the road? Cerys felt like she was about to explode. There were at least ten big Zulu women in the minibus, each taking up two people's space. They chattered to each other in shrill voices, the strange staccato clicks of the language flying over Cerys's head like noisy grasshoppers. Normally she liked hearing people talk Zulu, but right now she couldn't bear it.

Cerys got off a stop early so she could use the payphone. She had a mobile, but it was without signal or charge much of the time. She half-walked, half-ran to Mrs Ndongo's place. The old woman saw her coming and gestured to the little red phone on the counter. As Cerys pressed the receiver to her ear, it seemed hours before she heard it ring. It rang one, two, three times…Her heart beat faster. Four, five times. Her dad answered.

'Hello.'

'Hi. It's Cerys.'

'Oh hello.'

Silence.

'I suppose you got the emails.' He sounded tired, she thought.

'Yes.'

'Look Cerys, the funeral's next Wednesday. I'd really like you to be here for it.'

Cerys was momentarily taken aback, she hadn't even considered that it would be possible to go back.

'…oh! Well…it'll probably be very expensive…'

'Any idea how much?'

'Well, I know someone who paid a thousand dollars for a last-minute ticket to France. So I guess it could be six or seven hundred pounds. It's peak season.'

There was a pause.

'I'll pay for it.'

Her turn to pause.

'Are you sure that's what you want?'

'Yes. I really want you here, Cerys.'

'Well, I'll have to check it out with the orphanage. But…if you want me to, I'd like to come.'

'Okay, see what you can do. Hang on, Mum wants to talk to you…'

Pause.

'Hi Cerys.'

'Hi.'

'It would be nice if you came home. Dad's having a really hard time…it would mean a lot to him.'

'Yeah I know.'

'Cerys, why don't you just come back here for good? You can't really want to stay in Soweto. You've been there a year already…'

'Mum!' Cerys was cross. 'I can't just up and leave like that! I have a whole other life here! And…they need me at the orphanage!'

'They managed without you before.'

'Well, maybe I like it here!…I've got to go, the money's running out.'

'Okay. But do think about it darling.'

Cerys marched back to the house and flopped onto her mattress, facing the concrete wall. Granny's death still didn't seem real. It was too far away; she couldn't visualise it. As for going home! In the whole year, it had never occurred to her, not even once. It was almost as though while Cerys was here, her life back in Wales ceased to exist. But as she turned the idea over and over, memories flooded into her mind. In Granny's field, throwing sticks for the dogs. Shopping in Cardiff with Nic. Mum's roast dinners. Pints in the local. Nights out with her friends. Daisies. Ants that didn't bite. Green. Real, living, thirst-quenching green.

Cerys wanted to go back, now, more than anything. But then she thought about the one million Sowetans who didn't have the option of going anywhere, and she felt selfish.

Granny's dead, she thought.

'Granny's dead,' she said. I should cry, she thought. Maybe if I cry I'll feel better. So she cried for half an hour, which made her feel terribly self-indulgent. She thought again about how lucky she was compared with so many people, compared with those kids she looked after every day. A violent crack of thunder split the air, followed moments later by the deafening sound of rain hammering on the iron roof. Cerys's thoughts pressed in on her, and she closed her eyes.

★

The next day, Cerys tried and failed to corner Jessica in the office. Two new babies had come in, and several of the kids were sick. The baby room was fuller than ever, and babies were crying all over the place. Finally, when most of the kids were asleep, Cerys confronted Jessica.

'My granny just died. My family want me to go back to the funeral.'

Jessica said nothing for a moment, and Cerys saw she looked worn out.

'Cerys, I'm sorry about your granny. But if you go, I don't know what we'll do…We've never been so busy. Maybe if I had more notice I could sort something out, but…'

The green Welsh hills, the roast dinners, the chance to properly mourn Granny – all these things which had seemed there for the taking – all these things faded slowly in Cerys's mind's eye, until they were a mere dot on the horizon. She'd been stupid to let herself be tempted.

She should have known.

★

'Dad? It's Cerys…I'm sorry, I can't come home.' Cerys hated herself.

'I want to come, really I do. But I just can't. Not at such short notice. Please, please understand.' *Please*…Cerys felt tearful. There were all sorts of things her father could have said, about how family comes first, about all that they had given her over the years. But he didn't, and she felt worse because of it.

'I'm so, so, sorry…' she whispered.

Cerys hung up and walked home, head down. She

threw herself onto her mattress and sobbed. She cried for Granny, who would simply have vanished by the time she next saw home, and for Granny's house, which would be sold. She cried for her family, who were pulling together without her to support each other, and for herself, alone in another hemisphere. She cried in anger at her unhappiness, for she knew she was lucky; so, so lucky. For the first time she was homesick.

What am I doing here? She asked herself.

I'm helping, right?

Brown Rice

Sally Jenkinson

The pan's already hot on the stove, so I use a Tupperware box that's on the side to bring some more water over from the sink. The rice I'm cooking has soaked up all the water I started with. Brown rice. I've been told it's healthier than white. I've never really understood this cooking rice business; I can't really tell when it's cooked. How can you tell?

It doesn't matter if I don't think I'm the kind of man who cooks rice (brown rice no less!); I've got to cook rice now and there's no changing that. I'm a rice-cooker.

I think back to earlier in the day, walking up the road to collect Emmy from school. The same mixture of dread and guilt that I get every week at this time, creeping up the backs of my legs. I'd drag my feet but I can't bear to make myself late for her. Her class is just emptying out, and for a few minutes it's just a sea of small people wobbling about in front of me. Suddenly her little amber face emerges from the surf, and she spies me at the gate, smiles, and waves. But it's her mum waving back at me and I'm so sure that I'll throw her across the playground with rage if she comes near me. Then she starts sidling over, shrugging her rucksack back onto her shoulder every seven or eight steps because it's too big for her little frame; she's got this grace that's all her, and my heart just melts onto the hopscotched tarmac.

'Hi, what're we having for tea?' she tweets, taking my hand. 'Melissa's having Coq au Vin because it's Bastille Day.'

I don't answer for a minute, because I don't know what we're having for tea, I don't know what Bastille Day is, and my six-year-old daughter just said cock. Melissa's mum is talking.

'...it's not Coq au Vin really, just chicken stew. I try to make the things we do at home relevant to their school work, but it's so hard to keep up. You know more than me, girls. We didn't learn about Bastille Day when we were at school, did we Mr Spencer?!'

When you were at school, I think, *I probably wasn't even born.*

'Ha ha, no, just how to do the bare minimum and keep out of trouble...' She doesn't say anything in response to my attempt at parent-humour.

'So what are we having for tea?' Emmy pipes up.

'Erm, brown rice and...peas,' I finish in a desperate attempt to emanate some kind of parental adequacy. It's like word association. Salt; vinegar. Rice; peas. It just tumbles out. Mrs-Melissa's-Mum smiles in recognition.

'Oh, is that because of Emmy's mother's West Indian roots?' she asks. Suddenly I'm validated, in her eyes, by Emmy's little semi-fro.

'No.' I'm being short now, because I can't be arsed with this. 'Emmy's mum is from Oldham. So anyway, we better get off and get cooking! Bye Melissa!' I smile genuinely at them, because I think I'm funny, and stride swiftly away.

'Dad,' says my lovely daughter loudly, when I'm sure we're still in ear-shot of Cock-O-Van, 'I didn't know you could get *brown* rice. Is it dirty?' Emmy you *shit*.

'You do know, Silly-Billy,' I say just as loudly, faking a laugh. 'It's the stuff we have with peas!'

'Oh, right.' She looks confused, and I can see images of Sunday's special fried rice wobbling about in her mind. I scoop her off the path and carry her in my arms so we can get away from anyone else who might be listening as she reveals my failure at fatherhood to all and sundry.

We have to stop at the shops on the way home, because she's all excited about rice and peas now, and having lied to her at the school gates in order to save face in front of people I really don't know or care about, I feel like I owe her a shot at it. Luckily they sell brown rice, and I also buy some kidney beans, because I know that much. Emmy asks me what the beans will taste like and I tell her honestly that I've always thought kidney beans taste like damp cardboard, but all manner of things can happen when you add a few spices, so we'll give it a go.

All the way home she's chattering in my ear about cocko-this and brown-rice-that. When we get home, I'm glad she wants to play in the front room so that I don't have to embarrass myself cooking it in front of her.

At the stove, I look down to see that the rice has boiled dry *again*, and it's all stuck to the bottom of the pan. I stare at it for a minute.

'Emmy?' I call into the front room.

'Hmmm?'

'Do you fancy going for tea this aft?' I don't really like McDonaldsy-type stuff that much, but luckily neither does she so we don't have *that* generic 'going out for tea' dilemma. But I know what's coming.

'Dad, will they have rice and peas?'

'Mmm hmmm, yes, of course…'

How the hell has my daughter become obsessed with Caribbean cuisine in the last two and a half hours? This is what you get for lying to your daughter to impress snotty, Prozac-riddled middle-class mums.

I seem to remember that there's some kind of Jamaican restaurant somewhere along Oxford Road.

'Okay hon, get your shoes and coat on,' I shout, scraping my failed rice into the bin, which I notice is already overflowing.

'Wait! Where are we going?'

'Umm, I don't know what it's called, it's on Oxford Road.' I hear her scampering upstairs. 'Emmy?'

I shrug, and decide to change the bin now seeing as she's arsing about. Five minutes later she clumps back down wearing her little City shirt, a pink tutu and some jelly beach shoes.

'Erm, Emmy you…' I trail off. It's July so she isn't going

88

to freeze. Also, I notice that she's put some clips in her hair and everything. I get the feeling it'd crush her if I told her she looks like a bizarre hybrid of Andy Cole and the tooth fairy.

'Okay matey, let's go!' I'm pulling my coat on, but she gives me a withering look.

'Dad, you can't go out like *that*. There might be a nice lady or something.'

I'm gutted that my daughter is already becoming ashamed of my 'sense' of style; but worse than that, she's obviously noticed I've been lady-less for a very long time. However she's right, there are bits of my doomed culinary adventure stuck to my t-shirt so I slope off upstairs to change it.

'Put a nice shirt on, mucky-pup!' she calls after me, giggling. She sounds so much like her mum that it scares me. For a few seconds I feel the beginnings of something resembling anger creeping up the back of my neck, then I remember that it's a six-year-old girl at the bottom of the stairs, and she just wants her dad to look nice, so I oblige.

On the bus, I tell Emmy to keep an eye out for somewhere Caribbean looking, because I can't remember exactly where we're supposed to get off. She sits on my lap with her fingers clenched tightly round the bell all the way through Didsbury, even though I tell her I don't think it'll be for a while yet. I notice she's frowning, and ask what's up.

'I don't know what to look for, for the restaurant.'

'Oh, well maybe the colours red, yellow and green like the flag. Or a sign saying Jamaican cuisiiiiine…' I say in a silly voice, and tickle her a little bit under her arms, but she still looks serious.

'What about brown skin?'

'Umm, well, mostly the people living in Jamaica are black, but I…I don't think everyone in the restaurant will be, really, umm…'

I'm floundering pathetically, I'm shit at this. Why didn't I see this coming?

'I've got brown skin, but you haven't, and you're the dad', she proffers, patting my face absent-mindedly. 'I think I turned brown by magic.'

'Emmy, no. You know it's because your mum is black, and you're mixed race.' She's staring at her shoes. 'Your mum is black and English, and *her* mum is black and from Nigeria, can't you remember her telling you?'

'No,' she says resolutely. Then, with heartbreaking decorum my baby girl exhales gently, stares pointedly out of the window for ten seconds or so, and starts talking about Balamory.

'Emmy,' I begin, but she battles on purposefully with her CBeebies chatter, and I can feel her little body is tense as hell against my chest so decide to leave it, for now. I wrap my arms tighter around her and kiss the top of her head, which feels pathetic but it's all I can think to do.

At the table, luckily they've got something vaguely rice and pea-ish, which I order a bit of for Emmy and some jerk chicken and salad for me. She decides she wants a cup of jasmine tea which I don't seem to be able to talk her out of, so we order that too and a beer for me.

The girl who takes our order is surprisingly patient, especially with the cup-of-tea palaver. Normally when we go out, people automatically treat Emmy like she's an E-number time bomb, and could begin tearing about the place at any moment. They also presume she only wants chips and ketchup. In actual fact, considering she's never really had the opportunity to go anywhere or experience anything, Emmy's got more finesse and is more adventurous than loads of girls my age that you can see out in the city on any given night of the week.

It's a warm night, and they've got the doors open and the place is full of chatter and bursts of laughter. That, and the unfamiliar cooking smells make for a real summer holiday ambience. Emmy beams at me across the little table, sipping her tea.

Halfway through eating, she needs the loo. She always does this, but all that 'why didn't you go before' bollocks is so dull and I can't really be bothered with it. It's a pain though, because we've left the table empty, so I hope they don't clear the plates. I'm just opening the toilet door when Emmy stops in her tracks. I tug on her hand but she doesn't budge.

'Dad, this is the Boys.' Here we go.

'Yes, but I'm not allowed in the Girls mate, because I'm a grown-up. You're allowed in here though 'cos you're titchy-tiny!' I go to scoop her up but she wriggles away.

'Well I'm not anymore, it's embarrassing.'

No, I think, *this is embarrassing.* There are blokes squeezing past us to get in the loo, giving me very funny looks.

'Okay, okay,' I back away, just desperate not to be arrested. 'You go in the Girls and I'll wait out here, just shout if you need me.'

Hanging around outside the Ladies toilet isn't really doing much for my 'trying not to get arrested' plan, and I don't know if somebody has complained about me or what, but the waitress who served us appears, looking concerned.

'I'm just waiting for my daughter,' I gesture towards the door. At that exact moment a clattering noise starts emanating from the loo.

'Dad! Dad, I can't get out! The lock's stuck, Dad!'

The waitress puts her hand on my arm, 'I'll go.' She hurries in and I hear snippets of conversation.

'Hello Chick, I'm Phoebe. I brought you your tea, remember? Press the latch down as hard as you can before you slide it… Well done, let's wash our hands. Ooh, nice clips…'

They emerge holding hands. Emmy is all blotchy from crying but doesn't run and cling to me straight away. We all walk back to the table with the two of them still hand in hand. It's not until we sit down that Emmy clambers onto my knee.

'Thanks,' I say to Phoebe, 'I'm not usually so useless.' *I am.*

'No, no I think it's ace that you two are even out together. My sister's fella never takes their kids out on his own, refuses to. I bet your mum is glad of a night off, eh?' She tickles Em gently behind her ear. Emmy scowls openly at her and she suddenly looks very aware that she's crossed the line.

'Sorry, it's just erm, every day's a day off for her mam,' I say quietly, with my hand placed surreptitiously over the one of Emmy's ears that isn't pressed onto my chest.

'Oh, I…I'm sorry, sorry.'

'No, no it's okay really. You weren't to know, thanks for your help.'

'I've, um, got to…' she gestures towards the kitchen and hurries off.

We eat the rest of our tea with Emmy sat on my knee. She's impressed with the rice and peas, and when I try some it's really quite spicy, so I have to say that I'm impressed with her. Phoebe keeps nipping back to see if we're okay and if we need anything. When she's taken the plates away, I'm sat sipping my beer, and considering moving somewhere hot so we can do this every night. I suddenly realise that Emmy's been quiet for ages. I look down and realise that she's fallen asleep, so I settle up and carry her out.

At the bus stop, I'm just checking the timetable when Phoebe appears. She's minus her pinny, and wearing a denim jacket so I presume she's finished her shift.

'Oh hi there, are you finished for the night?' I ask, utching my lead-weight of a daughter up onto my shoulder. Outside the context of us being waitress and customer, I'm not sure if it's okay for me to just strike up a conversation with her, but she seems okay with it. She did rescue Emmy from a toilet after all. She answers that she's finished early, and her boss here is much nicer than where she used to work, and where do I work? Before I know it we're chatting away, and she's really, well, *interested*, asking questions about Emmy and stuff. I mention that she was really good with her in the loo and apparently she's the eldest of five herself, so is used to such crises.

I take a proper look at her; she looks a bit younger than me but doesn't act it. Her hair is scruffy and a bit greasy from the kitchen, but even so she looks good. For the first time in years possibly, I'm imagining what she'd look like across a table from me in a nice bar, when Emmy starts stirring. I can't help feeling a tiny bit disappointed. She sits up and looks around.

'Oh, I wanted a pudding,' she mumbles.

'I wanted to buy you one matey, but you conked out on me.'

Emmy makes that whingey-child noise which means she's too tired to make a proper fuss, but not tired enough to let it go.

'Well, I'm going to get a coffee,' Phoebe says. 'There's a café that stays open all night round the corner. You, well, we could get some pudding there…?'

I'm a bit flustered at first, then giddy all of a sudden, because I think this girl is asking me (us?) out, which has never happened before. Emmy, perceptive as she is, doesn't seem to have picked up on this, but mumbles something about cake. I look down at her. Her eyes are pink and sleepy, and the hand that isn't round my neck is gently patting my chest. Intermittently, she makes little grabs at my shirt, then lets go. She's always done this when she's dog-tired, ever since she was really tiny. My heart sinks predictably, but I can't ignore it. I'm a rice-cooker, well a rice-buyer at least. I'm getting there. I take a deep breath.

'That sounds great, but I'm really sorry we can't. It's a school night for us! I ought to get her to bed.'

She nods in understanding. We say polite, awkward goodbyes and she disappears round the corner.

'I wanted a pudding,' Emmy mumbles, but before I've even finished my school-night spiel, she's fallen back to sleep. I look at her, crumpled against my chest like a favourite teddy. There are no cracks between her body and mine. We fit together perfectly.

'It's just you and me from now on, Button,' I whisper, shifting her as gently as I can in my arms so I can fish some change out of my pocket for our bus home.

The Things I Learned About Leah Today

Sam Duda

Thursday 28 June

She is perhaps an A cup. They are not very big. It is the first thing I notice when we shake hands. This does not matter. The other day Jackie told Heather she was a C cup and hers are far too droopy.

She has smooth hands and she doesn't bite her nails, at least she hasn't for a while.

She tries to make jokes. This is good. They are not brilliant, but perhaps she is a little nervous.

She is slim and tallish.

She has nice eyes.

She has dark brown hair (the colour of a dark chocolate digestive biscuit).

A bad mouth (big, like mine, but on a much smaller face). I would guess her parents are not too worried about image, otherwise she would definitely have been made to wear a brace.

She has not mentioned a boyfriend.

Geordie.

Friday 29 June

She does not smoke.

The women in the office say she seems like a nice girl. Jackie made a joke that I should ask her out. I think it was a joke. It must be. I have only known this girl for one day.

She does not like dogs, but she quite likes a pub that allows them, as long as they are well behaved.

She lives with another girl, but there has been no talk of a boyfriend.

Twenty-five years old. We were in the same year at school, but obviously in different cities.

She is a little splay-footed and she walks a bit like a penguin.

Her breasts are bigger than I first thought.

Tonight she is going to watch a film with a friend. The friend is female.

Monday 2 July

She is a little jug-eared. I only noticed because she wore her hair back today. She has a pretty neck, however. Her skin is nice. Like milk.

She had a fun weekend. She watched *Jaws* on Friday with her friend. Apparently it is one of her favourites from childhood. I told her it was one of mine too, and she seemed pleased. I must watch it again to remind myself of some of the good bits.

She is smartly dressed. Her trousers amplify her nice buttocks.

Today she wore a good-looking pair of shoes. They

were like moccasins. Last week she wore spats and I thought they were stupid.

Her surname is Fletcher.

No mention of a boyfriend yet.

Tuesday 3 July

We walked home together today. I found out she lived on Sidney Terrace, which is two minutes from me, so we walked back all the way.

She doesn't look like a sweater (someone who perspires, not a pullover).

Her mouth is better than I first thought. The teeth give her character.

Her eyebrows are neither thick nor thin, with no sign of a potential monobrow. This makes it unlikely, despite the darkness of her colouring, that she will grow a beard when older.

Her younger sister studies chemistry. This is good if I ever meet her family. I am always worried that I would not have something to talk about.

She loves *Neighbours*, but I don't know her favourite character. She mentioned Harold and I laughed like a bird, high-pitched and twittering, but she didn't look at me strangely. Some people do when they first hear it.

She has very nice breasts.

She passed her driving test second time. On the first occasion she failed her parallel park.

Her dad has a season ticket at Newcastle.

She once won a sandcastle building competition on the beach at Tynemouth as a toddler and her photograph was in *The Newcastle Chronicle*.

She is not religious, but she believes there must be something. She likes arts and crafts, especially jewellery making, and she likes to ramble in the countryside. This is a good sign. Her previous dislike of dogs worried me, but this has made up for it.

Wednesday 4 July

Jackie made a childish ooooh noise when I told her that we had walked home together yesterday. It is sometimes hard to believe that these women are in their forties, the way they act.

Her voice is soft.

She bought me a bottle of water and refused to take my pound. I must remember to return the favour.

Her teeth are almost cute-looking. Like a little animal or something.

I saw her belly button through her blouse when it rucked up a bit. Good news. It is an inny.

I heard her tell Brenda that she liked a man with broad shoulders. I'm sure she must have noticed that my broad shoulders are my best feature.

Thursday 5 July

Today I was reprimanded by Caroline because my minutes contained too many errors. She said that it was unlike me and asked if I had other things on my mind. I said I did not.

Leah made me a cup of tea. It was too milky, but it was a nice gesture.

She sat with me for a while and we had a chat. Apparently Jackie was using the phone at her desk.

She is sceptical about global warming. She thinks it is a government controlling device.

She is a vegetarian, but this is okay. You can always change a woman, especially on food matters.

I noticed that she is slightly stooped and could do with spending some time improving her posture.

She went travelling after university, which is something that people often do with a partner. But she has still not mentioned a boyfriend. I am beginning to wonder whether she has ever had one.

Friday 6 July
I caught her looking at me three times across the office. The first time she smiled at me, the other times she looked away. Her face went a bit red and she definitely looked embarrassed.

Jackie told me at the photocopier that I looked smart and asked me if I had asked Leah out for a date. I pretended I did not have a clue what she was talking about. But now I am worried she will tell Leah that I am not interested. Not that I am, but I don't want to limit my options.

She has a nice laugh.

Her body is a perfect size and shape.

She told me that she likes ten pin bowling so perhaps she is a bit of a geek, but then I heard that she has been on a speedboat, so she is an adrenaline junkie too. I just cannot work this girl out. She is very enigmatic.

She has been watching the snooker. We spoke about Peter Ebdon.

She likes spinach and ricotta lasagne. There is an Italian restaurant on the road that lies between our houses.

Monday 9 July

Did not really see her today. She had a doctor's appointment and left early. I think it is a bit poor for her to be missing work this early on. She has only been in the office a week. I haven't taken a day off in the two years I have been there.

However, she did ask me whether I wanted to do a quiz with her on Thursday at The Four Feathers. I said I would think about it.

Still no mention of a boyfriend, but she is in a team which includes her sister's boyfriend's housemate. She pulled a funny face when she said his name. His name is Dan. I hope she is not shaping me up to be a friend she can tell about her love life. Frankly I am not interested in that.

Tuesday 10 July

I didn't ask about her health problem, but I did notice on the way home that she was red faced and sometimes short of breath. Perhaps she is asthmatic. I do walk quickly. I must remember to slow down a little.

She wore flip-flops on the walk home. They made an irritating noise, but she has nice feet. They are hairless, without sinew or unwanted bulges, and her toes are roundish. I wonder how she dances.

She leaned in front of me in the office and her hair smelled like flowers.

She has full lips.

Her eyes looked even better today. I think she had put some special make-up on them. And it looked like she had some sparkly glitter on her cheeks.

I told her that I would do the quiz. I will try to bring Kevin along.

It is *112* Sidney Terrace.

Wednesday 11 July

She liked my new haircut.

Her cheeks were sparkly again.

I told her my favourite parts of *Jaws* (I watched it over the weekend and memorised some of the lines) and she clapped with delight.

Her teeth are good for her face. It just works.

When we left each other she patted my back and told me that I better be at the quiz tomorrow.

Her quiz team is called *Burn Baby Burn*. I'm not sure what I think of this. It is a little naff, perhaps, but it sounds good when she says it with her accent.

On the way home she told me she is allergic to bee stings and that there are only five people in the world that know that.

Thursday 12 July

She beat me in the quiz. But only because she was in a team of six and I was with Kevin, who left at half-nine.

She wore a low-cut top and I noticed that she was leaning all over this Dan. He looks a bit rough. Short hair and I think he has an earring.

She drinks vodka.

I'm really not sure about the low-cut top.

Made no effort to be friendly at the pub. None at all.

Friday 13 July

She looked happier than usual today. It made her teeth look rubbish again.

We walked home together, but she was quiet.

After a while I stopped asking questions and we walked in silence.

Monday 16 July

I have forgiven her for her behaviour at the quiz. Perhaps she was a little drunk and showing off.

She wore a skirt today.

She has a freckle on her left knee. I like it.

Her legs are good and toned. Must be the rambling. We must get out into Northumberland for a walk soon.

She said she would lend me *Jaws 2* on DVD.

Tuesday 17 July

She didn't turn up for work.

Wednesday 18 July

Told me she was going to a job interview with some charity. Hadn't realised she was a do-gooder. Should have guessed with all that vegetarianism and arts and crafts.

Went over to make myself a cup of tea and stood near her desk, but she didn't look up. She must have known I was there, though. I coughed loudly two or three times.

Thursday 19 July

She got the job. She leaves tomorrow.

She is just a fucking quitter.

Friday 20 July

She made me a cup of tea. I let it go cold. When she asked why I hadn't drunk it, I told her that her tea was rubbish, but she just laughed. I said I wasn't joking, but she just laughed again.

After that she made a joke about one of the bananas in the fruit bowl and the women laughed. It wasn't funny. It was smut.

She went to the toilet seven times today. Maybe it is her time.

Walked home with her, but I was quiet. I wanted her to know. When we parted she wished me good luck and kissed my cheek. She told me she had enjoyed my company and that she was *sure* she would see me again. It sounded like a promise.

I waited outside for a bit. I didn't see a light go on.

Saturday 21 July

I think her room is at the back of the house. Her window was open.

She washed her hair and then wrapped it in a towel so it looked as though she was wearing a turban.

She dances quite well, but she listens to terrible music.

She went out at about three and didn't get back until ten.

Sunday 22 July

Saw her in the newsagents. She was buying bacon and marmite.

I told her that my parents died in a car crash last year. She seemed genuinely upset. She touched my arm and her skin was cold. It felt good and I thought about her hands as I was falling asleep.

Her legs look so tight in her trousers and I can imagine that her nipples are nice and pale, just like her skin.

Monday 23 July

Got her number from the system and called her at lunch from a payphone outside the office. She didn't wait long before she hung up.

Tuesday 24 July

Spoke to Mum today. She asked if I had met anyone and I hesitated. She started up with all sorts of questions, so I just said that it was too early for her to get excited. I said it was just a couple of dates. I said her name was Leah and she had nice dark hair and she was quite tall.

I did not mention the teeth.

Wednesday 25 July

Got up late and did not make it to work until ten. Jackie told me that Leah had been in earlier because she had left her coat or her bag or something. I must have gone red because Jackie made that bloody ooooh noise again.

I was in trouble again with Caroline.

This Leah bitch is really messing me about. She needs to get on with her own life, and leave me to get on with mine.

Thursday 26 July

Went to The Four Feathers and watched her flirt with that Dan. He looks brain-dead.

She drinks like a fish. She could not control herself when they won the quiz.

She kept making stupid woofing sounds when they got an answer right.

Walked back home with her, but so she could not see me. I wanted to make sure she was safe. I stayed on the opposite side of the road. She looked over once but I was definitely in the shadows.

Friday 27 July

I phoned her mobile with the intention of seeing whether she wanted to go out for a drink tonight, but panicked when she answered. Realised I was breathing down the phone too heavily, so I hung up.

She was out in the evening. Her housemate didn't know when she would be back.

Her window was shut.

(Her housemate has straight red hair, green eyes, and bracelets that jangle when she moves.)

Saturday 28 July

Not in. Her housemate has a nice silhouette.

Sunday 29 July

Bottles in her garden first thing. Perhaps she had a party last night. Did not get an invite.

I waited just down the road from her house. Sat on a bench and read a bit. She came out about midday. I saw her from a distance and walked towards her, pretending not to notice her, but she saw me and crossed the road to ask how I was. I told her I felt a bit down because it was the anniversary of my parents' accident. She said she was sorry, but left soon after.

She didn't touch my arm this time.

Monday 30 July

Took a day off work today. My first in two years. I think they owe me that.

Leah left for her do-gooder work at half-eight. Her housemate was gone by ten.

Found out that she leaves her window open. It is an easy climb up the shed. I am pretty sure it was her room. Those ridiculous spats were under her desk.

She shares her bed with a glove puppet.

I found some tissues in her bin.

Scratched her *Jaws* DVD with a pen.

Brushed my teeth with every toothbrush I could find in the bathroom.

Got that Dan's number from a list on the wall. Phoned him from their house and called him a twat.

Tuesday 31 July

Used a tissue to wipe my nose that I stole from her bin. It smelled of flowers. Just like her hair.

Wednesday 1 August

She is not a loyal friend. I phoned her from the office and she did not seem happy to hear from me.

I made a joke. *Pinch, punch, first of the month*. She didn't react. Nothing.

I told her that I felt trapped, that I needed some company. I asked her if she was free to meet up, but she said she had plans. I asked her about tomorrow and she just muttered something about that bloody quiz. How important is a quiz when one of your friends has lost his parents?

I told her I had found a lump. She told me to see a doctor and then the phone went dead.

I am not an idiot. She did it on purpose.

She is a heartless cunt.

Thursday 2 August

She left for The Four Feathers with a couple of *Burn Baby Burn* or whatever the fuckers are called. That Dan was there. He linked her arm when they crossed the main road. She let him.

She had a cigarette in the pub.

She had the low-cut top on.

She went to the toilet and when she came back she sat next to that Dan with his skinhead and his earring and his stupid big fucking face. She drank four drinks.

I think they only came third in the quiz, but they did win a bottle of wine.

That Dan gave her his phone and she came outside to make a call.

She was surprised to see me. She tried to leave, but I

asked her questions, told her I had missed her. She said thanks, but said she was so glad to have left my work. She couldn't believe that I had managed to stick with it for so long.

She made an excuse to leave and I started to follow her, but soon gave up.

Friday 3 August
It is the weekend again. Maybe I will see what she is up to.

I really must speak to her.

There are things she should know.

The Fruit Fly

Chris Killen

[illegible] her [illegible]

[illegible]

[illegible]

[illegible]

[illegible]

smoking [illegible] and they [illegible]

[illegible] her [illegible] get [illegible]

[illegible] through [illegible] like [illegible]

pregnant [illegible] them thinking [illegible]

[illegible]

Who runs away in a skirt, in October? Who runs away, full stop? Well, Carly Peach does; stood on the hard shoulder, feeling ridiculous, sticking her thumb in the air, only a burger and a few swigs of vodka inside her, and a pain in her heel. She stood on a pin. It went right in. She had to keep her mouth screwed closed, to not shout FUCK, or they'd've all woken up and found her.

She doesn't feel real. She feels like a story someone would tell you at school. Did you hear about Carly Peach? She's the one who ran away. She tried to hitchhike to her nan's in Scotland but the police caught her.

She's already a story at school, though. Did you hear about Carly Peach? She's pregnant. No shit. Dave Stockton knocked her up. I caught her puking in the bogs from morning sickness.

If only Angela Salmon knew the truth of it – that she'd been puking cuz she spent all night worrying and smoking fags and swigging Smirnoff. And that Dave Stockton came on her leg, before he could get it in.

It's weird, though. Secretly she likes the idea of being pregnant: she likes them thinking she's done it, even if it's made her life a misery, even if it's why she's freezing her arse off, stood here with her thumb in the air like an idiot, not going home ever again.

I'll wait all night, she thinks.

She has twenty quid.

She's fucked if she's catching the train.

Darren should never have broken the radio. He could be listening to something now. But it was Carol's fault really, for never shutting up. She'd been going on and on, playing with the dial, turning it, turning it, not shutting up, not settling on one station or another, so he'd taken her cup of Starbucks from the holder and dashed it over her hand.

The fingers scalded red.

She yelped.

The radio fizzled and died.

Finally she shut up.

She'd cradled her hand in her arm, scowling, but he'd been able to hear it still, going on inside her head: I want a baby, I want a baby, Darren. I want a baby.

Christ, Caroline.

He rubs his neck, and thinks of the smooth, skirted arse of Sarah Hobson, sat in front of him, fifteen years ago. He'd wanked himself off during Maths, from the pocket of his school trousers. She'd never known.

The lights are coming on.

The sky's greying.

It's Saturday.

And then something wonderful happens. He sees a

figure stood at the side of the road – a girl with long black hair in a skirt, slim, pale, her thumb stuck in the air. He peers at her as he passes, already touching the brake. It is. He can't believe it. It's bloody Sarah Hobson (from Maths) running towards him in the rear-view mirror.

He winds his window down; she leans in, hair hanging in her face, exactly the same. He wonders if she still recognises him.

Carly's had to be quick: she's had to make up a false name. But when she says it he says, no it's not. It's Sarah.

Fucking weirdo. He keeps looking at her, smiling, asking about school – whether they still have this teacher or that teacher – and she doesn't know what he's on about really, she just says yeah, or no, or whatever, thinking at least she's in a car and it's warm and she's moving.

If she had to guess, she'd say he's thirty.

He has this red rash that creeps from his collar. It curls behind his ear. He's stopped talking, but he's grinning still and biting a flake of skin from his bottom lip. You can see stubble on his cheeks. You can see it growing out from the rash.

Carly listens to the wheels. She closes her eyes, feeling bits of burger bob on the sloshing vodka-orange-squash in her stomach. Music would make it better. She doesn't want to think of Sam or Mum or Dad just yet.

So she asks, mind if I play the radio?

Be my guest, he says.

She clicks the dial, turns it between her fingers, but nothing happens.

Carol will be checking the clock. She'll have tea on. It doesn't take four hours to buy some cans of paint from Do-It-All. He gets his mobile out of the glove compartment, checks it – nothing yet – and turns it off.

He was just driving, anyway, before he picked her up.

Sarah Hobson's asleep, mouth open, head lolling. He knows it's not her, but it might as well be. She has the same freckles, same hair, same teeth. She even has that same sullen, cut-short way of speaking.

The smell of her is drifting across.

He wonders whether she has a baby. He wonders what her arse would feel like if he pressed the two cheeks together and bit into them.

She says she's going all the way to Edinburgh and he's promised to give her a lift to the next services. But then she's fallen asleep, and he doesn't want to let her go so he's driven past one exit, another, and now he's on the M6 following signs for Glasgow.

When Carly wakes it's night. She'd been having a dream about Sam – he was grown up, wearing one of her dresses, swinging it at the knees like a fashion model. His face was made up but he still had his short, six-year-old hair.

What time is it, she asks. Where are we?

Then she sees the clock on the dashboard: 20:09.

Are you hungry? he says. You were asleep. I'll buy you something, if you want.

She doesn't say no.

So they stop for burgers at the services. He pulls in and parks. A silence. They listen to the sound of the engine whining and cooling.

Don't you need to be home or something, she says, feeling her voice go strange at the end.

No, he says, leaving it at that.

They get out the car. He's shorter than she imagined. Stocky, thick-legged; she realises now what a fully-grown man he is. This isn't Dave Stockton, without a hair on his chest. As she stretches the ache from her back she feels her shirt ride up and cold air on her belly. She catches him looking, across the silvery blue roof of the car. A part of her feels sick. A part of her doesn't mind it.

As they walk towards the entrance she puts a swing in her hips. Behind her his eyes are on her arse.

Sarah Hobson (who claims her name's Samantha Something) will just have fries and a Coke, thanks.

Darren buys a Big Mac.

They take a corner table by the window. She keeps the straw in her mouth, running it round with her tongue.

Carol will be scraping dinner into the bin. She'll be standing in the hall, the phone against her ear, listening to that answerphone message he recorded in Ibiza, pissed, wondering if he's been in some sort of accident, and whether she should stick the news on or take a tablet and go to bed.

There's a family sat a few tables away, the only other people in here: a man, a woman, two sulky children. The man's looking over. Darren starts to feel shifty.

Where were you planning on sleeping? he asks her.

She stops rolling the straw. It drops from her mouth. She looks up, narrows her eyes, and sharp lines appear at their edges. Black eyes, they are, with dark purple underneath.

Dunno, she says.

His hands have gone clammy. His neck's started to prickle.

Why?

It's dangerous isn't it, a girl out by herself like this? Got any money?

A bit.

Does your family know where you are?

Yeah.

It isn't going to work, she's not gonna go for it, but fuck it, he decides to ask anyway: how about we stop off at a hotel? It's late. I'll pay. And then tomorrow I'll drive you the rest of the way.

She puts a couple more fries in her mouth. Chews. Swallows. Looks from him to the family and back again (the man's gotten up for the toilet).

Darren scratches behind his ear, not breathing.

Alright, she says.

Back goes the straw in her mouth.

The hotel room is warm. Darren's gone to the bathroom, having a piss; she can hear it through the door. Carly sits on the edge of the bed, her toes not quite touching the carpet. There is just the one bed in here – a double. He made her wait in the car while he booked it. The window's open: a black stretch of night outside. Everything is so quiet. You can see the car park.

She begins writing a letter to her brother in her head, from ten years in the future:

Dear Sam,
Hope you're okay. I'm doing well. The weather here is great and you'll have to come and visit sometime. Sorry I ran out on you, but I'm glad we can finally talk about it now, and that you're not pissed off at me…

Then the toilet flushes and Darren comes out, the ends of his hair wet. He walks round the room, not looking, like he's thinking or wanting to say something. He has his shirt undone. She can see curls of hair on his chest. He sits down, still not looking at her, and starts to put on his shoes.

What is it? she wants to ask.

She says nothing.

I'm going to the bar.

Standing, he buttons his shirt.

Be back in an hour or so.

The room is silent. Perching on the edge of the bed, wondering what she's doing, is Carly Peach. She's not going home. A man who smells of sweat and aftershave has gone to the bar. He's coming back in an hour. He says his name's Darren and he drives a blue Vauxhall something-or-other and she should have remembered the number plate. There's only one bed in the room.

Two couples sit in the bar lounge: one laughing and drunk, the other not making eye-contact.

Darren's in a corner swigging Stella.

He imagines Samantha What's-Her-Face still on the edge of the bed, swinging her feet, not turning on the telly. She gets up, and floats around the room brushing her fingers over the laminated menu and the tea-making things, and in the bathroom the free soaps, shampoos, hand towels. She walks to the door, opens it, sticks her head into the hushed red corridor – and it is as simple as that. The door's open. She's free to put on her trainers and click it closed behind her whenever she wants; there's nothing he can do about it.

He puts his hand in his pocket. A bit of loose change, his car keys, some toilet roll.

If I go back and she's still there, he decides, then she wants it.

It won't be illegal.

He thinks of Carol (who'll definitely be worried by

now). He should've made up a lie. I bumped into an old friend out of the blue, or, there was this accident and I had to stick around after to tell the police.

An accident, he'll say. It was all an accident.

Right. Finish his pint. Go to the car. Give Carol a call. Then, if she's still there…

Does a candle count? Carly Peach doesn't think it does. A human being, she clarifies. She's never done it with a human being before.

She gets up, and floats around the room brushing her fingers over the laminated menu and the tea-making things, and in the bathroom the free soaps, shampoos and hand towels. She turns on the shower and tries the water. Just right. So she locks the door, undresses, gets in.

Running shampoo from her hair she remembers how Sam used to stand in the bath to let her wash him. His little dick, more skin than anything else. He'll be gay when he grows up. Sam Peach with a missing sister. Once she's settled she'll come and rescue him.

Carly dries herself. Idiot. She didn't even bring a spare change of clothes. She was never any good at planning ahead.

So she just puts on her knickers and vest (not her bra) and gets into the bed, deep under the covers. She closes her eyes. She waits a long time. She turns off her bedside light. He should be back any second. In the dark, the smell of the hotel shampoo and the hotel soaps are like they're coming from someone else.

It is this someone else, not Carly Peach, who suddenly begins to speak to her:

I wait a long time with my eyes closed, they say. Even when I hear the door go, I don't open them. He brings a cloud of fags and lager in with him. The noises he makes are too loud: creaking shoes, rough breathing, a jangling belt. He's taking off his trousers. Now he's unbuttoning his shirt. I can hear each button slip softly through its buttonhole. I can hear the tick of his watch against the wooden night table. I can see his bare shoulders, the occasional pimples on them, even with my eyes closed. He pauses and looks at me. He doesn't say anything. The bed creaks. He pulls off the covers. I lay still, keeping my eyes shut.

Don't move, I say to myself. His hands are hot. They pull down my knickers. Don't move and don't look, I say to myself, but I spread my legs a little bit for him. His hands move to my knees, to push them further apart. He sticks in a finger. God. It feels as if one finger is all you could ever fit in there. He moves it in and out, in and out.

Don't move, I say. Don't look at him and don't make any sort of sound. But I bite my lip and hiss from my nostrils. He takes out his finger, shuffles between my legs so his belly's brushing mine, and he's breathing hard now, smelling of fags and sweat and aftershave. He's licking his lips, grinning like a demon: his face all red, I can see it even with my eyes closed. Then it goes in. A sharp pain. Fuck. It feels like I'm going to split in two. I bite, I hiss, I want to throw my arms round him, but I keep them at my sides with my fingers clenched in balls. It only goes in a bit at first, it feels so hot and big and long that it's all the way up in my stomach. Then he pushes it further and further and further so I want to scream. Oh god, I want to scream. Oh god, oh god, oh god…

Carly hears a sound. Her hands freeze between her legs. Her eyes shoot open. It's a sound from the car park: a rattling engine. She pushes back the covers, jumps out of bed, and rushes to the window not wearing her knickers, knowing already what's happened.

She's right.

From the second floor she sees a yellow arc of headlights, and then the back end of Darren's blue Vauxhall as he drives through the car park exit, going and going and gone.

A Christmas Outing (in February)

Alex Wire

[illegible] A Christmas Outing (in February)

[illegible]

[illegible]

[illegible] if [illegible] been [illegible] about [illegible]

[illegible] direct [illegible]

[illegible]

'So who's going to be at this thing?' he's saying.

'Well,' I say. 'There'll be my boss, Keith.'

'The editor?'

'Yes, the editor. And Hayley and Liz from the features team, and the news desk – that's Phil, Mark, Kris and Sanj – a few people from IT whose names I can never remember which is why my computer hardly ever works, a couple of the sports team, Geoff and Luke I think, Debbie from reception, maybe a few of the freelances and…'

And my boyfriend.

'…and, err, that's all I know.'

Not that I've ever called him that at the office. My 'partner' is how I've tactfully – tactically – put it.

'Well I can't wait to meet them all,' he's saying as he straightens my collar and thankfully he doesn't really look at my face which I'm sure is wearing a dumb grin.

Straight people use that term too nowadays, I know. It's not as if I've been overly evasive about it. I just haven't been particularly direct either. Not dishonest, but perhaps not entirely honest either.

'Come on, we'll be late,' he calls from the hall and I

hear the jangling of car keys being retrieved from a glass fruit bowl that's never seen an orange in its life. 'Stop daydreaming. I imagine your boss is quite keen on punctuality, what with deadlines and all that, and I'm *determined* to make a good impression, even if you aren't.'

It's not as if straight people arrive at a new job and go, 'Hello, I'm Paul and I'm as straight as a Roman road,' 'Nice to meet you; my name's Dave and I only like girls too.' It just wouldn't be normal to greet a group of complete strangers and instantly disclose what it is you like doing and doing to you in bed. 'Hi, I'm John and I like to dress up in gimp outfits and be whipped by French maids.'

I follow him out of the flat and he pinches my bum as I go through the door. 'Cheer up,' he says. 'It's supposed to be Christmas.'

'It's February,' I say through the cold air.

'Bah! Get in the spirit, Scrooge!' he yells as the door clicks shut.

It's like those questions about your health on the application forms. You're supposed to be as honest as possible, list all your embarrassing ailments, in case it later affects your work and puts your contract in doubt. But no one ever is totally honest because there's a good chance the prospective boss might give the job to someone whose guts don't turn to sewage at the merest taste of cheese, has narcoleptic fits whenever they look at a computer screen or often has to spend days at a time in bed with depression. It might put you in a difficult situation at a later point, but you're still better off keeping it quiet in the moment.

'Humbug,' he says as I climb into the passenger seat of his Fiesta.

'What?'

'Would you like a humbug?' He's holding out a bag of the stripy sweets.

'What are you like?' I say and give him a peck on the cheek while my hand forages in the bag. 'Can you even buy these this time of year? Or have you been saving them up for that joke?'

'Of course you can buy them, love,' he says as he starts the car. 'Prunes on the other hand...'

He does make me laugh.

Does it put your friendship with someone at risk if you haven't told them you're gay within a certain number of weeks? Would I be pissed at any of our gay friends if they turned out to be straight and they hadn't told me? You know what, I probably would. And that makes me a horrible hypocrite. But our gay friends are our *gay friends*. We're probably only friends with them because they're gay. Their gayness is part of who they are to us. What if my gayness is part of who I am, a part I've been keeping secret? Oh no – that makes me an even bigger hypocrite!

'Any idea what the parking's like at this restaurant?'

'Shit,' I say.

'I hope we don't have to walk too far in this snow – it

will ruin my new suede shoes.' And then he gives a little Elvis-style Uh-hu-huh.

God, I love this man. He makes me laugh so much!

Yes, I suppose my gayness is part of who I am, but it doesn't define me. Is it really a big deal if everyone thinks it's Nikki n i k k i and not Nicky n i c k y? Does it matter all that much if I pretended to myself not to hear when someone inquired about my 'girlfriend' or 'the missus'? If, on a Monday morning, a colleague asks what I got up to over the weekend, they want to hear about us going kayaking down the river or visiting my parents, not some dramatic revelation about my sexuality. It doesn't matter to anyone.

And if it does, well fuck them! That'll be their problem. It's not going to change things between me and Nicky. We're together and in love – that's what's important. And...

'Just down here, isn't it?'

I haven't even noticed but we're in the town already.

'Yes, and then the next left,' I say.

And then we are pulling up down the road from the restaurant and stepping out into the cold, snowy air and I'm wondering why I haven't told Nicky that they don't know, and I'm no longer worrying what they will think of us but what *he* will think of *me*.

He says something I can't quite hear.

'The only what?' I say.

'WAG. You know, Wives-And-Girlfriends, like the

footballers have. I'm not going to be the only one there, am I?'

'No, of course not. Most of the other hacks are married. I expect they will have brought their wives.' I'm trying to sound casual, relaxed.

'Ah, so I might be the only girlfriend then,' he says, and for a moment I wonder if he knows what I've been thinking, knows what I've done. But he's grinning cheerfully.

'Gavin!' calls Keith as we walk in. He comes over from the bar to meet us. 'Gavin – nice to see you.'

'You too, Keith,' I say, shaking his hand and thinking, you saw me at the office this morning.

There's an awkward pause as Keith notices Nicky.

'Introduce us then,' says Nicky.

'Erm, well this is Keith, my editor.'

'I've heard a lot about you,' says Nicky, shaking his hand.

'And this is Nicky,' I say.

'Nice to meet you, Nick,' says Keith in his warm country brogue, giving him a manly slap on the arm. 'Say, Gavin, I thought you said you were coming with your par...'

And there it is. The realisation. I see it first on Keith's face, then Nicky's.

'Ahh, I see!' says Keith.

I shrug a tiny, apologetic shrug.

But then, and I'm not expecting this, Keith says, 'Well you better come meet the rest of the rabble I call my newspaper,' and he's leading Nicky off to the bar where about twenty assorted journalists, sub-editors and their WAGs are milling around, chatting and laughing. I'm almost left behind as Keith introduces Nicky to the rest of the group as 'Gavin's partner' in his booming, genial voice. My face is burning up red. There are a few moments of hesitation among the others. I catch the sports team giving each other quick glances. But Nicky is in the middle of the mêlée shaking hands, exchanging nice-to-meet-yous.

'What can I get you lads to drink?' calls Keith from the bar.

'Oh – a lager please,' says Nicky. 'Thanks!'

My throat is dry and I croak out, 'Glass of white wine, please.' And then I feel embarrassed because my drink order is more gay than my boyfriend.

'So how long have you been together?' Sanjay's wife is asking.

'About a year,' I say. I knew the conversation was going to turn to us eventually, once alcohol helped curiosity overcome politeness.

'And you live together, is that right?'

'Yeah,' I say.

'Gav moved in with me when I opened my new practice.'

'Oh, are you a doctor?'

136

Gav laughs. 'Well,' he says. 'I'm a doctor as far as the local cats and dogs are concerned.'

My throat tightens as I wonder if he's going to make his usual, terrible Gay Vet cracks: I've chopped off more balls than I've felt up; most people in the gay community have a different idea of dogging; I've met some cats in my time…

But thankfully he doesn't go there. There is for our gay friends only.

Actually, so far Nicky has been a complete hit, cracking jokes and listening patiently to the shop talk. And I'm starting to wonder what I was afraid of. Prejudice? Hell, it's a newspaper. A provincial paper, maybe, but a newspaper nonetheless, and journalists tend to be open-minded people. Bitter and heartless, sure, but open-minded all the same.

'Any plans for a wedding?' says Paul's wife who is the most tipsy of the WAGs.

Nicky laughs and I blush into my wine glass. I'm sure I can see the redness of my cheeks reflecting off the crystal.

'Not yet,' says Nicky. 'We're not quite ready to make honest men of each other.' And everyone laughs.

'Say,' says Keith, who has been lording it up all evening as the convivial host (shame he's not paying for us all though), 'who does the proposing in…that kind of marriage?'

'The bravest,' says Nicky and the table cracks up again.

Nicky's only had the one pint of beer because he's driving, so everyone else is a little drunker than him, but he's funny anyway. He's really funny. That was what first attracted me to him, I think. I remember when we first met, at a friend's party.

'Hi, you're Gaz, aren't you?' he said to me at the bar. 'One of Tony's friends?'

'Gav,' I said. 'Vvv.'

'Ah sorry. Sometimes I get the wetters mixed up in lerds.'

'I bet that can be quite embarrassing,' I said.

'Oh yes. Only the other day I asked a waitress for a cup of pee and a slice of ghost.'

That doesn't even make sense! But at the time I thought it was hilarious. Hilarious enough for us to swap phone numbers and a bit of saliva that evening.

'Well Gavnin...' This is Geoff, shouting down from the far end of the table in a slurry voice. He's had a skinful. He thinks he can take his beer, it's part of his all-man image, but really he's a worse lightweight than me. 'You kepd all thisth pretty quiet. But, hey, there's nowt wrong with ith in my books. And to be honesth, I alwaysh suspecthed you were a bit that way inclindeded sinsh you were so keen to report on the local drama group'th production of the Wizard of Oth!'

Everyone looks awkwardly at me and Nicky, but he's laughing and everyone else realises it's okay to laugh. That kind of gay joke is okay. It's near the line, but not over it, and a gay man is laughing so it's okay the same way as when black people tell racist jokes about fried chicken and fat mommas. I think.

'Well, Geoff,' I say, trying to join in, 'Dorothy and I are good friends so it would have been rude not to go see her.'

Nicky touches my leg under the table as everyone laughs – he's pleased for me that my joke was funny and wants to share the moment with me, which means he really loves me, I reckon.

The waitresses are starting to clear away the table. I glance round the restaurant and realise that our raucous behaviour has cleared it. I'm glad because what's coming next is going to be embarrassing. Keith is tapping the side of his beer glass with his fork and pushing his chair back so he can stand.

'Now folks,' he says, 'I know it isn't the most traditional thing to have your work Christmas dinner in February. But in our trade needs must and I'm sure you'd rather be sitting here now than working on Boxing Day because we were behind on that week's edition. I remember a time in 1987 when...or was it 1989? Hmmm...Well it doesn't matter because working late one Christmas Eve is as unpleasant as working any other. But I'm sure you'll agree that tonight has been marvellous fun and it is really positive for the paper if we all get to know each other out of the office...' and I switch off because I've heard this speech recited a dozen times by the other staff members; it's the exact same speech he gives every year at the February Christmas dinner, a popular in-joke. I hear him mention something about 'learning a bit more about each other, some more than others' and a few people chuckle, but my attention is fixed on the ridiculous big white cake being wheeled towards the table. The words *Camp as Christmas* appear in my mind.

'They seemed like a lovely bunch,' Nicky is saying as we drive out of the town. The snow's falling hard now and the windscreen wipers are crunching in a slow rhythm.

'Yes, they are,' I say.

'You must have quite a laugh at the office.'

'Sometimes.'

I feel him glancing over at me. 'Anything the matter, hon?'

'No, I'm fine,' but I know I don't sound it.

'I'm not mad at you, you know.'

'What do you mean?'

'For not telling them. You probably expected me to be mad when I found out you'd kept me a secret, but I'm not. I understand.'

'Yeah?'

'Of course. I mean, I don't go telling all the pet owners that come into my surgery that I'm gay. I'm sure it wouldn't make the blindest bit of difference and they don't care who gets their hands on their animals, but there's still no need for me to tell them.'

'I bet you've told your colleagues though.'

'I have a picture of you on my desk. They kinda guessed from that.'

'Exactly.'

'But two veterinary nurses is hardly the same as a testosterone-filled newspaper office.'

'I suppose not.'

'I wouldn't have told them if I were you. Wouldn't know how to broach the subject, to be honest. But you took me to the meal and that was a really brave thing to do.'

'Hmmm,' I say, trying to sound affirmative.

'And everything went well so there's not a problem and, honestly, I'm not mad in the slightest.'

I should have known that Nicky would understand. I don't know why I didn't trust him not to get angry.

But instead of feeling relief, I just feel wrongness. It all feels wrong somehow. Maybe I wanted there to be a problem after all. Maybe I wanted him to get angry. I don't know. I had this whole disaster scenario worked out in my mind and for some reason I wanted it to come true just because it was what I had been expecting. And maybe I wanted everyone at the office to be shocked and appalled, to take offence at my dishonesty and be sickened by my abnormality. Maybe I wanted the evening to be an embarrassing mess and for me and Nicky to argue in the car home, for him to say, 'You should have told them! How do you expect people to react if you just spring it on them like that?' and then we'd get home and talk it over and have make-up sex and vow that it wasn't going to affect our love, that the problem was theirs, that we would battle our way through the prejudice and it would only bring us closer together. We would be bound by adversity. Maybe that's what I wanted to happen. And maybe I'm upset because it didn't happen. Maybe I needed it to happen. And maybe that means Nicky and I aren't as bound together as I thought.

'Humbug?' he's saying, waving the bag of sweets in my general direction. I reach to take one, hoping the sugar will stop my head feeling so dizzy.

This Is Not a Road Trip

Amanda Rodriguez

We are headed south. Some people would call this a road trip but this is not that. Road trips are for people who have time to burn. Two Lips has got a couple of weeks, they said, maybe a month at best. And you don't say no to a dying friend.

The music on the radio, the voice of our so-called generation, concerns itself with getting large-breasted women even more naked than they already are. 'Why do you listen to this crap?' I ask Two Lips, who is a large-breasted woman herself. Or was.

'Because I *like* it, okay? It's catchy. And this is *my* trip.'

She turns up the music and it shakes the loose metal of her shitty car with each low bass thump. Why do I keep talking? I can't seem to open my mouth without criticising her. But I can't do it. I can't shut up and relax, because I am being driven by a drunkard in a shitty car with old tyres that hasn't seen an oil change in god-knows-when, and this music is going on and on about the same shit that got Two Lips into this situation in the first place.

'It's degrading.'

'Look, bitch, when you're driving I'll let you pick the music, all right?' Two Lips turns it up so loud that you can't even hear the words anymore, just the thump of the bass and its vibrations through the rusty metal and up through the bucket seats. 'Come on, Pix, you know you like that bass.' She raises one eyebrow at me, mischievous, flirting. Two Lips doesn't know how to turn off the sex, even now, when she weighs about ninety pounds and all the colour is gone from her face. 'Oh, Pix!' she yells over the music. 'That bass! I think I'm gonna...' she grabs my knee and moans, throwing her head back and pretending to come. The car weaves left, over the centre lane.

I laugh at her even as my heart jumps into my throat and we narrowly avoid oncoming traffic. 'All right, Miss Lips, come all you want, but just keep your eyes on the road while you do it.'

'Really?' she asks me, doing the eyebrow thing again.

'Yes. Really.'

'Okay!' she says, and throws herself into moaning again. This time, though, the car stays in its lane.

We are passing mountains. Two Lips has never seen mountains before in her life. That's what you're supposed to do when they tell you you've only got a couple weeks left to live – if you're young and you know in advance, that is – which is not common but it's the situation she's in.

You're supposed to live every day as if it's your last, but of course that's bullshit, because then nobody would take out their trash or have a driver's licence or do any of the thankless jobs that they have. So when you haven't lived every day as if it were your last, then you do what Two Lips is doing, which is living the last three weeks of her life as if she could pack in every moment that she always wanted to have. This involves a virtual pharmacy in the trunk, thumping music to shake the seats, and mountains.

What I don't know is when she plans on stopping. Unlike Two Lips, I did some research on the line that we are travelling – a straight line down in the Sierra Nevada – and it's pretty much mountains all the way down. If she wants to see the tallest one on the continent, then we're going the wrong way. We are burning gas and money, and there are all of these mountains all around her. I mean, I know, it's not supposed to be about the destination, it's supposed to be about the journey, and really I shouldn't worry so much because Two Lips has got five credit cards that she fully intends on charging to their maximum limit. You don't worry about good credit when you're dying, which is another way that the whole idea of living every moment to its fullest is totally bullshit. Regular people, people who are not Two Lips, do not spend ten thousand dollars in three weeks without thinking twice about it, unless their last name happens to be Hilton. Of course, though, she deserves it; she deserves to have the entire national budget in her pocket. But even that wouldn't make up for the sixty years of her life that have just slipped through her fingers like some sick magic trick. How much would you sell a year of your life for? Like the MasterCard commercials say: some things are just priceless.

Two Lips starts coughing really hard and we get off the road just in time for her to hang out of the car window and puke her guts out on the shoulder of the road. I try to be sympathetic, but it's got to be a lot nicer to spend your last days in enough of a state of sobriety that you're not puking up Kettle One and diner omelettes every few hours, right? When she's finished I try to scold her, but she cuts me off before I can even get a word in. 'Yes, Pix,' she says, wiping her mouth with a napkin from the glove box, 'I will now lay off the vodka. And you can drive.'

I roll my eyes. 'How very generous of you, Lips, thanks a bunch. Just drive up a couple of feet so I don't have to walk in your puke, okay?'

'Right-o.' She drives further up the shoulder, and we both get out of the car to switch places. I look at her as we pass each other in the front of the car. She looks so much smaller when she's not driving, smaller than I've ever seen her before. I think of what she used to look like, when we were teenagers. She used to be a big girl. Not fat, but with lots of steep curves that made everyone stop and stare at her. Two Lips had literally caused traffic accidents just by walking down the street; and this at a time when the supposedly beautiful girls were those who called a celery stalk dinner. The fashion magazines could say what they wanted, but tits had never gone out of style and Two Lips never let anyone forget it.

I get into the driver's seat, trying to ignore the puke that was sprayed down the outside of the car door. Two Lips takes the passenger seat and immediately falls asleep. She's been sleeping a lot lately. I start to drive, not knowing where to go except straight ahead. I figure we will stop when she says so, and she isn't going to say so for a while, at least. I turn off the radio and watch the mountains roll endlessly by.

Three hours later Lips wakes up, scaring the shit out of me when she speaks. 'Pix.'

'Yeah?'

'What would you do? I mean, pretend you're me. Only a little bit of time. What would you do?'

'If I were you?'

'Yeah.'

'No one is anything like you, Two Lips.'

She smiles. 'Okay, you're you.'

I've thought about it. Of course I've thought about it. How could I not? Still, though, I've never come up with anything that's remotely satisfying, some plan that would make it okay, after three weeks, to just keel over and leave everything behind. 'I don't know, Lips,' I say, 'but I'd want to spend it with you.' That sounds worse than the songs on the radio, but it's the only thing that I know for sure.

She smiles at me. 'Thanks.'

We're quiet, then, watching the mountains and the sun that's going down, making it all look like we're driving into a postcard. Two Lips and I don't have to talk about how beautiful it is — we both just know it. We're from the same flat place filled with the brown apartment buildings that blend in very well with the grey sky, and the cold that never seems to go away for long enough. When Lips and I were growing up, in one of those brown apartment buildings, we used to get these giant coffee table books from the library about Art Deco buildings on Miami Beach and tell each other about how we were going to get two of those houses, right next to each other, and spend all day tanning on the beach. This trip is the first time that either of us has seen anything even remotely like this. I mean, Midwestern farms have their charms when the light is slanted just right, but it's nothing like *this*.

It makes me sick, now, watching it roll by, knowing that there's no way to make it stop, and no way to speed it up either, to somehow get her all over the world so she could see every mountain and every beach. How many mountains could she see in sixty years? Almost all of them, or at least enough that she would have her fill, that at some point she would say, 'All right, Pix, I've had enough of the goddamn mountains now.' But instead I've got to watch her staring out the window as if she's eating every last one and she can't get enough and I can't give her any more.

I pull the car off the road to get some gas. Lips goes in, to get some coffee, she says. There's an old guy in the next pump over filling up his truck that stares at her as she walks into the store. Even weighing about as much as a nine-year-old boy, Lips has got the walk that makes people stare at her. I wonder, not for the first time, if I am in love with her. I'm not gay, but I've never met a man in my life that makes me ache the way I do for her. I mean, that old guy thinks he's in love with her, but he hasn't spent the past twenty-three years of his life with her, like I have. You would have to be an idiot not to love her.

I go in to pay. Lips said that she would pay for everything, but I don't want her to. I don't know where we're going but I want her to have a five-star hotel and room service when we get there. When I get into the store, Lips is already charging everything. We go back to the car and Lips says she wants to drive again, so I get into the passenger seat.

I must have fallen asleep then, because when I wake up it is under another set of fluorescent lights in another gas station, and everything around us is black. Lips has already filled up the tank and is pulling out of the station, back onto the nearly deserted road.

'Hey,' I say, shifting in my seat. My back aches from sleeping cramped up in the seat.

'Are you ready?'

'For what?' I see only blackness, no sign of any civilization except a few distant, twinkling lights.

'Just wait,' she says, and I do. She turns the car off the highway and we get onto a smaller road. The windows are down a notch so that when she pulls off the highway, I know what it is without asking, because I can smell the salt of it. And there it is, staring back at us from beyond the lamplights of a deserted parking lot.

'The ocean,' she says, simply.

'God, Lips. It's pretty huge.' I can't say anything else. I keep waiting for a finite end; I want this to be that moment where we are so overwhelmed by the beauty of this thing, the ocean, that we can both be satisfied and think to ourselves, 'All right, that's it, now we can leave forever.' But this ocean isn't it, not right now. It's pretty, of course, with the moon reflecting down in a big white line across the waves. But this isn't it; and I am beginning to think that that moment just never exists, that there will always be the possibility of more. We get out of the car and walk across the abandoned parking lot to the beach, and sit down in the sand. It's warm here, at least, and we take off our shoes and put our toes in the sand. Lips stares out at it, hugging her knees.

I know that it's selfish of me, but I want her to say that it's okay. But the unwritten rule is that you're never supposed to ask. We just plunge straight into the future, because that's all that any of us knows how to do, and it's what we're supposed to do. I want her to tell me that it's okay even though I know it's not, because I'm terrified. I've never known anyone who was dying before, except my grandfather, and that was a long time in coming. My grandfather died at the time in his life when people are supposed to, and all of the light had gone out of his eyes. But Lips is still burning strong. She is going to go, I know, without ever having any of the light fade – it's just going to be smashed out of her, one second burning strong and the next just gone.

'Let's build a fire,' Lips says, and I try not to get freaked out that she's just answered my silent metaphor.

'All right,' I say. 'We'll need flashlights to get the wood.'

We go back to the car for the flashlights. We have to dig around a bit through the stuff in the trunk to get at them. Lips grabs the little bag that she's been using as a travelling pharmacy, too, and pulls out a few of the prescription painkillers that the doctors gave her.

'Want one?' she asks me.

You're not supposed to take these kinds of pills unless you're old or terminally ill or just a young kid trying to get some kicks, and I really want us to be in that last category. 'Sure,' I say, and swallow the pill with water from the gallon jug that I insisted that we keep in the trunk for emergencies. Two Lips takes two.

We head out to the beach again and start collecting driftwood and twigs. It takes us about forty-five minutes before we've got enough gathered in a huge pile, and then we go about stacking it up. 'God, I think the last time we did this we must have been twelve, right?' Lips asks me. 'Girl Scout camp.'

'Yeah,' I say, 'let's see if I can remember how, because I know *you* weren't paying attention.'

'Hey!' she feigns indignation.

'Oh, come on, you spent the whole time composing love letters to Jimmy Frandon.'

'Well, Miss Pix, I am about to show you that I am a woman of many talents. I am capable of both wooing a man and learning how to stack up a pile of logs. Watch.'

I do. Lips expertly puts in all of the twigs and piles up the larger pieces, teepee-style, and then lights it up with old twisted newspapers from the car. In a few minutes, the fire is huge and glowing. 'Told you!' she says, triumphant.

The drugs have kicked in, hard. I wonder if Lips is feeling the same sort of euphoria that I am. 'They gave you some good drugs, at least,' I say.

'Yeah, they are pretty good, huh?' she says, smiling and poking at the fire with a long stick. 'Two is just right.'

We stare at the fire she has built. It feels good to be sitting here with her, next to the ocean that neither of us has ever seen before, next to a fire. The fire is strong and mesmerising. Maybe it's the drugs, but staring at it and listening to the ocean crash up on the beach is making me feel calmer than I've felt in a really long time.

'God, it's better than television, you know?' says Two Lips.

'I know. It's like the first television,' I say. 'I mean, just think about how long people have been watching fire, just like we are.' I pause and then start laughing.

'What?'

'Oh, nothing, just that that sounded so *deep*.'

Lips giggles and puts her arm around my shoulder. I realise that there is not a thing about this moment that I want to change. It's warm, the ocean is spread out before us, and Two Lips is smiling. I can't tell her that, though, because saying it would make it go away. So I change the subject. 'Whatever happened to Jimmy Frandon, anyway?'

'Oh, he was a perfect gentleman,' Lips smiles, pouring sand on her feet. 'He never made his move. That's why I went for Kyle Mulligan.'

'Oh god, that's right!' I groan, 'He was so disgusting!'

Lips laughs and pretends to make out with the air, rolling her tongue around violently. 'It was just like that!'

'Should have waited for Jimmy,' I sigh.

'Yeah,' she says, 'if there *is* a Heaven then I will be presented with a harem of Jimmy Frandons the second I walk through the gate.' I know she's kidding but jokes about the afterlife are not really something that I can handle right now, and it pierces through the drug euphoria and makes my heart race.

Two Lips knows it and covers it by joking more. 'I'm sorry, I shouldn't have said that,' she says. 'I mean, the whole point of a harem is variety, right? Fuck, it's *Heaven*. They'd have to throw in a few Matthew McConaugheys and maybe Antonio Banderas, too. And Steve Urkel.'

'What?!' I laugh. 'Steve Urkel?' Urkel was the nerd in highwater pants from *Family Matters* that we used to watch together as kids.

'You've always got to have something for comparison, to remind you of what you've got,' she says. 'You wouldn't want to take all of those Jimmy Frandons for granted.'

'You are a strange, strange woman, Two Lips.'

Lips smiles at me, the huge crooked Two Lips smile that's caught god knows how many men in its trap. That smile is how Lips got her name, because when she does it the rest of her just disappears and that's all that there is. Just two lips. I feel euphoric again, and hug her. The fire is strong and glowing in front of us.

'I feel kind of tired,' she says, then, 'too much driving.'

'Yeah, me too,' I say, lying. 'Let's go to sleep.' She lies down in the sand, and I lie down next to her, my eyes open, staring at the stars.

'Hey, Pix?' she says in a whisper.

'Yeah?'

'If you come with me, I'll let you have Urkel.'

I force myself to laugh. In a few minutes, Lips is snoring softly next to me. I get up as quietly as I can and walk back to the car with one of the flashlights, the pavement rough under my bare feet. I open the trunk silently and get out her medicine bag and the gallon jug of water and bring them with me back to the fire. I pour out her bottle of prescription pills in my hand, and stare at them. I look over at Two Lips. She's still sleeping, quietly, the fire lighting up her face. I swallow the pills, one by one, until there are only two left. Two will be enough for her, for tomorrow, and she can get more if she needs them. I lie down next to her and stare at her sleeping. I want to tell her that she's beautiful, that she's the best person that I've ever known, that she is the person with the brightest light, that I love her, that she deserves five thousand harems of Jimmy Frandons. But none of it seems big enough. I lie down and put my arm around her waist and my head on her shoulder. The fire is cracking loudly and the light is everywhere.

'Lips?' I say. She stirs and says something like 'ummmmm.'

'I'll take Urkel.'

'Okay.' She smiles and turns over. I smile too, and close my eyes, letting the light go out.

Contributors

Catherine Browne

Born: 1981, Blackpool

Lives: Leeds

Currently listening to: The Ting Tings, Black Kids, Orchestra Baobab.

Currently preoccupied by: I'm both anxious and excited about the changes I'm making to my life.

First memory: is aged three, at my little brother's christening; my dad is taking a picture of us and my Great Uncle Jack is pretending to pour a cup of tea on his head to make us laugh.

Currently annoyed by: shop assistants who stand around chatting to each other whilst you're waiting to pay.

Favourite books: Nabokov's *Lolita*, Fitzgerald's *The Great Gatsby*

Favourite places: Paris, Berlin, Whitby

When you're not editing, what else do you do: bake cakes, drink tea, climb hills.

Katharine Coldiron

Born: 1981, Charleston, South Carolina, USA

Lives: Maryland, USA

Currently listening to: Jonathan Coulton's folk-rock cover of 'Baby Got Back' (look it up!)

Currently preoccupied by: yoga

Where else can we see your stuff: kcoldiron.blogspot.com, *very* occasional updates. Google me.

First memory: being scared to death on Santa Claus's lap at the age of four.

Currently annoyed by: the Supreme Court

Favourite place at the moment: my sofa

When you're not writing, what else do you do: I like to knit, think, read.

Christine Cooper

Born: 1983, Doncaster

Lives: Leeds/Sheffield

Currently listening to: kitsch electro pop music, especially Chinese kitsch electro pop music. Oh, and English country dance tunes.

Currently preoccupied by: whether art should be free; the meaning of nationhood; our impending doom; other diverse topics too numerous to mention...

Where else can we see your stuff:

www.youtube.com/watch?v=Z_SnuETj-G4

www.myspace.com/theislandersband

When you're not writing, what else do you do: I am a storyteller in the very literal sense, in that I go to schools, museums, festivals and firesides, and tell stories to the people there. I am a folk musician in the sense that I travel and bring music to people in pubs, village halls, schools, on mountainsides...

Sam Duda

Born: 1982, Norfolk

Lives: at present I live in Cornwall.

Currently listening to: Beirut, Fionn Regan, and Vetiver.

Where else can we see your stuff: in an anthology called *You Interrupt My Brain, Sweetheart* and in Chimera magazine.

First memory: is of me, aged four, on a beach, white-haired and naked, running up to people and grinning at them, wearing plastic joke-shop vampire teeth. One old woman recoiled in horror and fell backwards over a dog.

Currently annoyed by: I would like to say the escalating price of petrol or the abolition of the 10p tax, but nothing gets to me as much as the lack of cricket on TV.

Favourite place: Prague

Favourite book: *What a Carve Up!* by Jonathan Coe

Favourite films: *Don't Look Now*, *Who's Afraid of Virginia Woolf?* and *A Room For Romeo Brass*

When you're not writing, what else do you do:
I like old rosie and the cover drive and the change from A minor to E minor.

Chelsey Flood

Born: 1983, Derby

Lives: Falmouth, Cornwall

Currently listening to: cars and seagulls. (Not a band.)

Currently preoccupied by: the growth of the sex industry in England, particularly the increase of lapdancing clubs (a new one opens every week, on average) and what this means for us all.

Where can we see your other stuff:

litflood.blogspot.com

First memory: having a go on a 'seesaw' my brother had made – it was a plank of wood held across a bar of our climbing frame – and him bouncing me so high I flew right over the top. I was fine but cried to get him the punishment I believed he was entitled to. I never know if this memory is real. Is it possible to go right over the top of a climbing frame? And be fine? I just don't know.

Currently annoyed by: the amount of unfinished stories in my laptop and what this says about me and my ambitions.

When you're not writing, what else do you do: daydream and nap. It's a problem.

Sally Jenkinson

Born: 1986, Doncaster, South Yorkshire

Lives: Sheffield

Currently listening to: this week…mainly 90s all-girl punk bands, traditional folk tunes, and a little bit too much Leonard Cohen.

Currently preoccupied by: Angela Carter, adventures and absinthe

Where else can we see your stuff:

www.writeoutloud.net/poets/sallyjenkinson, the Camina Poetry Journal and the *Obsessed With Pipework* magazine.

First memory: asking my mum to look after my pork pie at a picnic, whilst I went off to play, and returning to find that she'd eaten it. I've forgiven her because aside from this small digression she is an astoundingly wondrous human being, and also because I've been a vegetarian for the past ten years so it was probably for the best.

Favourite word at the moment: I can't stop thinking about the word 'deliquesce'.

When you're not writing, what else do you do: support people with learning disabilities; read on trains; paint; eavesdrop on strangers' conversations; camp and/or drink gin.

Chris Killen

Born: 1981, Kenilworth, Warwickshire

Lives: Chorlton, Manchester

Currently listening to: right this second: The Unicorns. Generally: Frankie Sparo, Les Savy Fav, The Smiths, The Shins, etc.

Currently preoccupied by: Canadian music (Frog Eyes, Wolf Parade, Sunset Rubdown, etc.), and films by Joe Swanberg.

Where else can we see your stuff: my first novel, *The Bird Room*, published by Canongate. I write a blog: www.dayofmoustaches.blogspot.com

First memory: something to do with a slide. A yellow slide. I'm standing at the top of the slide, and my dad's trying to fix it, and I'm laughing at him for some reason.

Favourite book and writer: *Pan* by Knut Hamsun. My favourite writer who was born in the 1980s is Tao Lin.

Luis Amate Perez

Born: 1982, Queens, New York

Lives: New York, NY

Currently listening to: Tool

Where else can we see your stuff: you can see me, sort of, on Facebook. Become my friend: http://www.facebook.com/profile.php?id=822184

First memory: it was a dream – or I was somewhere between being asleep and awake. I was probably three years old. I'm lying in my parents' bed, and above me is floating a baby bottle filled with orange juice. I reach up to grab it.

Favourite thing at the moment: the work of George Carlin. In short, he was one of my gods.

When you're not writing, what else do you do: check out some of my comedy at www.GregandLou.com

Amanda Rodriguez

Born: 1980s
Lives: rural Mexico

Gareth Storey

Born: 1980, Dublin

Lives: Camden, London

Currently listening to: N.E.R.D, Shellac, Talking Heads, Lovage, Martha Wainwright.

Currently preoccupied by: women

Where else can we see your stuff: myspace.com/whoisatmydoor

First memory: riding an elephant

Currently annoyed by: people who don't say 'please' and 'thank you'.

Favourite thing at the moment: *Curb Your Enthusiasm*

When you're not writing, what else do you do: work in a kitchen, exercise, drink, read, eat, watch films, clean and sleep.

Alex Wire

Born: in Worcester in 1983, several weeks late, allegedly.

Lives: Nottingham

Currently listening to: Johnny Flynn, Dan Le Sac Vs Scroobius Pip and Elbow. Not at the same time, but if it's possible I'd like to try it.

Currently preoccupied by: the actor Lionel Barrymore.

Where else can we see your stuff:

www.sparkle-and-believe.blogspot.com

Favourite book at the moment: the plays of Pinter and the poetry of Larkin.

When you're not writing, what else do you do: chastise myself for not writing, play guitars, imbibe culture, drink to remember.

Other Route Books

The Train of Ice and Fire
Ramón Chao
ISBN: 978-1-901927-37-5
Hardback price: £14.99

Colombia, November 1993: a reconstructed old passenger train, bespangled with yellow butterflies, is carrying one hundred musicians, acrobats and artists on a daring adventure through the heart of a country soaked in violence. The intention is to put on free shows for locals at railway stations along the way: vibrant spectacles involving music, trapeze, tattoo-art, an ice museum and, star of the show, Roberto the fire-breathing dragon. Leading this crusade of hope is Manu Chao with his band Mano Negra.

Ramón Chao is on board to chronicle the journey. As the train climbs 1,000 kilometres from Santa Marta on the Caribbean Coast to Bogotá in the Altiplano, Ramón keeps one eye on the fluctuating morale of the train's eccentric cargo, and the other on the ever-changing physical and social landscape. As the papa of the train, he endures personal discomfort, internal strife, derailments, stowaways, disease, guerrillas and paramilitaries. When the train arrives in Aracataca, the real-life Macondo of *One Hundred Years of Solitude*, Mano Negra disintegrates, leaving Manu to pick up the pieces with those determined to see this once-in-a-lifetime adventure through to the end.

The Train of Ice and Fire is a book about hope and dreams in troubled times. It is about a father accompanying his son through an experience which will change his life. But most of all it is about Colombia, the flora, the fauna, the history, the politics and, more than any of that, it is a book about people.

Bringing It All Back Home

Ian Clayton

ISBN: 978-1-901927-35-1

Paperback price: £7.99

When you hear a certain song, where does it take you? What is the secret that connects music to our lives? Heart warming, moving and laugh out loud funny, *Bringing It All Back Home* is the truest book you will ever read about music and the things that really matter.

Author Ian Clayton listens to music as a kid to escape and as an adult to connect. In *Bringing It All Back Home* he has created a book about love, friendship, family and loss – about life and living it. While searching for a soundtrack to his own life story, he has discovered the heart that beats inside us all.

Made In Bradford

Editor: M Y Alam

ISBN: 978-1-901927-32-0

Paperback price: £8.99

The aftermath of the Bradford Riots in 2001 and subsequent reports on how the city is constructed, provoked novelist and academic M Y Alam into generating a report of his own. As part of the research process, he spent time interviewing British Pakistani men and gathered their views on issues which are generally prone to misrepresentation elsewhere. Over a period of time these sessions became much more than the usual researcher and research subject kind of relationship. In some cases, they developed into full blown conversations amongst friends.

Made In Bradford compiles a series of transcripts from those conversations and paints a vivid picture of everyday life that reads almost as a counter-narrative to the prevailing direction of current debates. Here, men talk about issues such as forced marriage, drugs and criminality, employment, racism, political representation, the fall out from the London bombings, faith and freedom, along with the notion of home and belonging. The openness within the texts is a refreshing antidote to the recent, more widespread and shameful stigmatisation of a people within our own communities. *Made In Bradford* is an important book of its time.

The Route Series

Route publishes a regular series of titles
for which it offers an annual subscription.

Born in the 1980s (Route 21) is a title in the Route Series.

www.route-online.com